"We can't be both friends and lovers, Kade!" Brodie protested.

"We can be anything we damn well want," Kade replied. "But for now, why don't we try to be friends first, figure out how we're going to be parents together without complicating it with sex?"

He confused and bedazzled her, Brodie admitted. She couldn't keep up with him. She felt like she was being maneuvered into a corner, pushed there by the force of his will. "I don't know! I need to think."

Kade smiled, stepped back and placed his hands into the pockets of his khaki shorts. "You can think all you want, Brodie, but it isn't going to change a damn thing. I'm going to be around whether you like it or not." He ducked his head and dropped a kiss on her temple.

"You might as well get used to it," he murmured into her ear.

* * *

Pregnant by the Maverick Millionaire is part of the series From Mavericks to Married—Three superfine hockey pl[illegible] finally meet their matches!

Dear Readers,

In *Trapped with a Maverick Millionaire* you met Mac, the first of my panty-meltingly hot, unfairly talented and commitmentphobic Mavericks heroes. This is Kade's story. I have to say that I have loved every minute of dragging these stubborn guys to the altar.

Kade and Brodie each have massive issues around love and happiness, and when they meet again after six months, the chemistry between them is off the charts. They agree to a onetime thing, just to work it out of their systems. After their fantastic time together, Brodie and Kade talk about the fact that Brodie has donated a free matchmaking session to be auctioned at the Mavericks' Charity Ball, and Kade tells her that he'd rather be shot than be "matched" by her.

Then their world tilts upside down. At the auction, Mac's fiancée, happy and in love, puts in a preposterous bid for Brodie's services and gifts it, very publicly, to Kade, in the hope that the "elusive one" will find his match. Kade can't refuse and Rory has donated the matchmaking session and life is suddenly very complicated.

And how exactly are you supposed to find a guy his life partner—even though he doesn't want one—when you are carrying his baby? And what do you do when you start having feelings for him when you aren't supposed to feel anything for anybody ever again? Read on to find out!

With love,

Joss

xxx

Connect with me at www.josswoodbooks.com

Twitter: @JossWoodBooks

Facebook: Joss Wood Author

JOSS WOOD

PREGNANT BY THE MAVERICK MILLIONAIRE

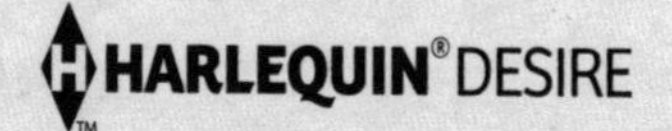

ISBN-13: 978-0-373-73476-4

Pregnant by the Maverick Millionaire

This edition published by arrangement with Harlequin Books S.A.

For questions and comments about the quality of this book, please contact us at CustomerService@Harlequin.com.

Printed in U.S.A.

Joss Wood's passion for putting black letters on a white screen is matched only by her love of books and traveling (especially to the wild places of southern Africa) and, possibly, by her hatred of ironing and making school lunches.

Joss has written over sixteen books for the Harlequin KISS, Harlequin Presents and, most recently, Harlequin Desire lines.

After a career in business lobbying and local economic development, Joss now writes full-time. She lives in KwaZulu-Natal, South Africa, with her husband and two teenage children, surrounded by family, friends, animals and a ridiculous amount of books.

Joss is a member of the RWA (Romance Writers of America) and ROSA (Romance Writers of South Africa).

Books by Joss Wood

Harlequin Desire

Taking the Boss to Bed

From Mavericks to Married

Trapped with the Maverick Millionaire
Pregnant by the Maverick Millionaire

Harlequin KISS

The Last Guy She Should Call
Flirting with the Forbidden
More than a Fling?

Harlequin Presents

One Night, Two Consequences
Her Boss by Day...
Behind the Headlines

Visit her Author Profile page at Harlequin.com, or josswoodbooks.com, for more titles.

One

Funny.

Built.

Sexy.

Smart. So, so, smart.

Courteous, hot, confident.

He was the entire package, a gorgeous combination of everything any woman would ever want or need for a flash-in-the-pan encounter. That being said, Brodie Stewart knew there were at least a billion women in the world who would slap her senseless for what she was about to do and she didn't blame them.

"Brodie? Did you hear me? I asked if you want to come upstairs," Kade whispered into her ear, his hand on her rib cage, his thumb rubbing the underside of her right breast.

She licked her lips and tasted him on her tongue, inhaled the citrus and spice of his soap-scented skin and tipped her head sideways to allow his lips to explore the cords of her neck. Man, he was good at this, Brodie thought.

She should step away, she *should stop this…*

She'd been saying the same thing for three weeks. She shouldn't have waited for Kade every early morning on the running trail, shouldn't have felt the butterflies in her stomach when he loped toward her, a six-foot-plus slab of celebrity muscle. She shouldn't have laughed at his jokes, responded to his gentle flirting. And she certainly shouldn't have accepted his offer to return to his place for a lazy cup of Saturday morning coffee/sex after their seven-mile loop around Stanley Park.

As much as she wanted to know what that cocky, mobile mouth could do, she definitely should *not* have kissed him.

She'd thought she had it all worked out, had convinced herself she could handle this, him. It wasn't like she hadn't had sex since Jay. There had been a few guys—okay, two—since the accident a decade ago. On paper, Kade was perfect. The ex-professional ice hockey player, now second in charge of the Vancouver Mavericks, was resolutely single. Proudly unavailable and, unlike most females of a certain age, Brodie had no desire to change him. In fact, one of the reasons she'd said yes to his offer for coffee was because she knew exactly what he wanted and it wasn't a happily-ever-after with her.

Okay, it had been a while and she was out of practice, but why, oh, dear Lord why, couldn't she get past her hang-ups and have a quick tumble with the gorgeous, very practiced Kade Webb?

Maybe it was because something about him resonated with her, because he was more than a pretty package. Because his kisses were deep and compelling and made her quiver with more than a quick physical connection. He reminded her of love, of intimacy, of emotional connections.

She really didn't want the reminder.

Brodie peeled herself off Kade's wide chest and dropped a quick so-sorry kiss on his chin, her lips brushing the golden stubble on his jaw. She rolled off the leather couch, stood up and walked over to the floor-to-ceiling folding doors leading to an expansive balcony. Brodie placed her hand on the cool glass. From this penthouse loft downtown he had the most amazing view of False Creek and the Granville and Burrard bridges. It was a big-bucks view and absolutely fabulous. She took it in…and gave herself time to form a response to his question.

Reluctantly Brodie turned and placed her hands behind her butt, leaning against the glass. Her heart and libido wanted to return to his embrace, trace those long, hard muscles, taste his naturally olive-shaded skin, shove her hands into his loose, surferboy blond hair, watch those brown eyes deepen to black as passion swept him away. But her brain was firmly in charge and it was telling her to run, as far and as fast as she could, before she found herself in a situation that was out of her control.

God, he was going to think she was a tease, that she was playing him. She wasn't, not really. She was just protecting herself.

Emotionally. Psychically. In all the ways she could.

Brodie felt his eyes on her but stared down at her sneakers, wishing she was wearing more than a tight hoodie and running tights. She knew he was waiting for an explanation for her blowing hot and cold, for kissing him senseless and then backing away. She couldn't tell him—this man she'd jogged with, who knew nothing more about her than her name and that she liked to run—that even though she was crazy horny, the idea of sex, *with him*, reminded her of intimacy and intimacy scared the skin off her.

He was supposed to be a fun time, a quick thing but, dammit, Kade Webb had stirred up emotions she thought were long dead. Of all the men in Vancouver, why him? He was such a cliché—handsome, wealthy, charming, successful. In Jane Austen's world he would've been called a rake and three hundred years later the moniker still suited him well.

Brodie sighed, wishing she'd played this differently. Everyone knew what a fitness fanatic he was, how fast he ran, and it was common knowledge that he ran most mornings in Stanley Park. She'd wanted to see if she could, in any way, keep up with him. Instead of keeping pace with him at the crack of dawn, she should've hung back and kept her distance. At first he'd been amused with her idea that she could match his long-legged stride, but she'd run track in college. She had speed and stamina on her side. When he realized he couldn't shake her he started bantering with her. Many runs and many conversations led to this morning's invitation for coffee/sex.

She'd enjoyed those random conversations so much she'd frequently forgotten she was jogging with the city's most elusive bachelor. To her, he was just a guy with a wicked sense of humor, a sharp brain and, admittedly, a very sexy body. Running alongside him had certainly not been a hardship. She'd actually taken pleasure in his appreciation of her.

So much so that she'd thought she was strong enough, brave enough, to have a casual encounter on a Saturday morning as any other confident, sophisticated, modern woman would. Yeah. Right.

"You've changed your mind, haven't you?" His voice was as rich as the sunbeams dancing across the wooden floor. Her eyes flew up to meet his and, to her relief, she didn't see any anger in his expression, just regret.

"I'm so sorry. I thought I could." Brodie lifted her hands in an I-don't-know-what-happened gesture.

"Was it me? Did I do something you didn't like?"

Aw…

Brodie blushed. "No, you're fabulous. God, you

must know you kiss really well and I'm sure..." Her blush deepened. "I'm sure you do everything well."

Kade pushed himself into a sitting position on the couch and placed his ankle on his knee. He leaned back and the muscles in his big arms flexed as he linked his hands behind his head, his expensive running shirt pulling tight across his broad chest. She could see the ridges of his stomach and knew the fabric covered a perfect six-pack of sexy-as-sin muscles.

Stop thinking about his body, his stomach, about those hard thighs...

"Maybe you'd feel more at ease if I tell you you're in control here. You say no—to anything, at any point—and I'll back off," Kade quietly stated.

This was a prime example of why she was attracted to him. Beyond the charm, beneath the sexy face and the scorching body, was the man she suspected the public never saw; someone who was thoughtful enough to put her at ease. Someone who could quiet her fears, who could make her consider casting off a protective layer or two.

Thoughtful Kade reminded her of Jay, which reminded her of the person she'd been before her life had been turned inside out. The open, happy, sunny girl who'd loved life with a vengeance. A young woman who had the world at her feet.

That was what scared her most about being with him. He made her remember who she'd been before she wasn't that person anymore.

Sex she could handle, but she was terrified of

feeling good, contented. She couldn't deal with happiness.

Not when she knew how quickly it could be ripped away.

Brodie bit her lip and lifted her hands in the air. She saw a hint of frustration pass across Kade's face.

"Okay, then I really don't understand. You seemed to be as into me as I am into you."

Brodie scratched the back of her neck. "Yeah, I'm a mess. It's difficult to explain but trust me when I tell you it's all me and not you."

Kade nodded. "Oh, I know it's all you 'cause if I had anything to do with it then you'd be naked and panting right now."

Well, there wasn't a hell of a lot to say to that. She should just go. "This was a very bad decision on my part." Brodie moved away from the window and clasped her hands behind her back. "I'm really sorry to blow hot and cold."

Kade stood up and raked his fingers through his hair. "No worries. It's not the end of the world."

She was sure it wasn't, not for him. He'd had a variety of woman hanging off his arm since he was eighteen years old and new to the Mavericks. In sixteen years, that was a lot of women and a lot of hanging. With one call, one text message, he could have Brodie's replacement here in ten minutes.

So, there was an upside to this stupid scenario; she would never be one of "Webb's Women."

As she walked toward the door, Kade's phone

buzzed and he picked it up off the coffee table. He swiped the screen with his thumb and frowned as he read the text message.

"Quinn and Mac are on their way up," he said.

Quinn Rayne and Mac McCaskill, Kade's best friends, his ex-teammates and current business partners. Yeah, she wasn't proud to admit that, like every other obsessed Mavericks fan, she read about their exploits in the papers and online. The women, although Kade wasn't quite as much a player as Quinn and Mac, the crazy stunts—mostly Quinn—the scandals… Quinn again. Actually, these days, it was mostly Quinn who gave the press grist for the mill.

Brodie glanced at her wristwatch. It was 7:36 a.m. on a Saturday morning. "So early?"

"Yeah, weird." Kade stood up and walked across the expansive loft to the kitchen area. He opened a huge fridge and pulled out two bottles of water. He waved one in her direction. "Want one?"

Brodie nodded and easily caught the bottle he lobbed in her direction. "Thanks." She gestured to the door. "So, I think I should go."

Kade nodded his agreement, saw she was struggling to crack the top and walked toward her. He took the bottle, opened the lid and handed it back to her. "There you go."

"Thanks," Brodie said and gestured to the couch. "Sorry, you know…about that."

Kade's expression was pure speculation. "Maybe

one day you'll tell me why." They heard a clatter of footsteps outside the door. "My boys are here."

"I'll get out of your way."

Kade moved past her and opened the door to his friends. Brodie opened her mouth to say a quick hello, but her words died at the looks on their faces. They pushed past her to flank Kade, looking pale. Their eyes were rimmed with red.

"What's wrong?" Kade demanded, his voice harsh.

Brodie watched as they each put a hand on Kade's shoulders. Her stomach plummeted to the floor at their expressions; she recognized them instantly. They were the bearers of bad news, the harbingers of doom. They were going to tell him his life was about to do a 180.

She'd seen the same expression on her aunt's face when Poppy had told her that her parents, her best friend, Chelsea, and her old friend but new boyfriend Jay were dead, along with six other people, in a nightmarish accident. They'd been on their way to a dinner to celebrate her twentieth birthday and apparently life had thought being the lone survivor of a multivehicle crash was a suitable gift.

Why was I left behind?

"Tell. Me." Kade's snap brought her back to his hall, to the three men looking like the ground was shifting under their feet.

"Kade, Vernon had a heart attack this morning,"

Quinn said, his words stilted. "He didn't make it, bud."

She saw the flash of denial on Kade's face, the disbelief, and she quietly slipped out the door. Grief was an intensely personal and private emotion and the last thing he needed was a stranger in his space, in his home. Besides, she was still dealing with her own sorrow, still working through losing her own family, her closest friend and the man whom she'd thought she'd marry.

Sorry, Kade, she thought. *So, so sorry.* A long time ago she'd had a brave heart and a free spirit and she hoped the news of his friend's death wouldn't change the core of who he was, like the same kind of news had changed her.

But life *had* changed her and she wasn't that free-spirited girl anymore. She walked back into her real life knowing she certainly wasn't the type of woman who could handle sexy, bachelor millionaires tempting her to walk on the wild side.

Six months later

Brodie typed her client's answer into her tablet, hit Enter and looked up. Dammit, she thought, instantly recognizing the interest in his eyes. This appointment was already running overtime and she really didn't want to fend off his advances.

This was one downside to dealing with male clients in her matchmaking business. Because she was reasonably attractive they thought they would skip the sometimes tedious process of finding a mate and go straight for her.

"What type of woman are you looking for?" she asked, deliberately playing with the massive-but-fake emerald-and-diamond monstrosity on the ring finger of her left hand.

"Actually, I was going to say a tiny blonde with a nice figure but I'm open to other possibilities. Maybe someone who looks like you…who *is* you. I have tickets for the opera. Do you like opera?"

Ack. She hated opera and she didn't date her clients. Ever. She didn't date at all. Brodie sent him a tight smile and lifted her hand to show him her ring. "I'm flattered but I'm engaged. Tom is a special ops soldier, currently overseas."

Last week Tom had been Mike and he'd been an ace detective. The week before he'd been Jace and a white-water adventurer. What could she say? She liked variety in her fake fiancés.

Brodie took down the rest of his information, ignored his smooth attempts to flirt with her despite her engagement to Tom and insisted on paying for coffee. She watched as he left the café and climbed into a low-slung Japanese sports car. When she was certain he was out of view, she dropped her head to the table and gently banged her forehead.

"Another one asking for a date?" Jan, the owner of the coffee shop, dropped into the chair across from Brodie and patted her head. Despite Brodie trying to keep her distance from the ebullient older woman, Jan had, somehow, become her friend. She rarely confided in anybody—talking about stuff and discussing the past changed nothing, so what was the point?—but Jan didn't let it bother her. Like her great-aunt Poppy, Jan nagged Brodie to open up on a fairly regular basis.

Funny, Brodie had talked more to Kade in three weeks than she had to anybody—Jan and Poppy included—for the last decade.

Well, that thought had barreled in from nowhere. Brodie rarely, if ever, thought about Kade Webb during daylight hours. Memories of him, his kiss, his hard body under her hands, were little gifts she gave to herself at night, in the comfort of the dark.

"Being asked out on dates is an occupational hazard." Brodie stretched out her spine and rolled her head on her shoulders in an effort to work out the kinks.

Jan pushed a pretty pink plate holding a chocolate chip cookie across the table. "Maybe this will make you feel better."

It would, but Brodie knew there was something other than sympathy behind Jan's fat-and-sugar-laden gesture. "What do you want?"

"My cousin is in her thirties and is open to using a matchmaker. I suggested you."

Brodie scowled at her friend, but she couldn't stop herself from breaking off the corner of the cookie and lifting it to her mouth. Flavors exploded on her tongue and she closed her eyes in ecstasy. "Better than sex, I swear."

"Honey, if my cookies are better than sex, then you ain't doing it right," Jan replied, her voice tart. She leaned forward, her bright blue eyes inquisitive. "You having sex you haven't told me about, Brodie?"

She wished. The closest she'd come to sex was Kade Webb's hot kiss six months ago, but sex itself? She thought back. Three or so years?

She was pathetic.

After taking another bite of the cookie, Brodie pulled her thoughts from her brief encounter with the CEO of the Mavericks professional ice hockey team and narrowed her eyes at her friend. "You know I only take men as my clients, Jan."

"Which is a stupid idea. You are halving your market," Jan said, her business sense offended. But Brodie's business model worked; Brodie dealt with men, while her associate Colin only had women clients. They pooled their databases and office resources. As a result, they were doing okay. In the hectic twenty-first century—the age of the internet, icky diseases and idiots—singles wanted help wading through the dating cesspool.

"Women are too emotional, too picky and too needy. Too much drama," Brodie told Jan. Again.

Brodie snapped off another piece of cookie and wrinkled her nose when she realized she'd eaten most of it. She was a sucker for chocolate. And cookies.

Thank the Lord she had a fast metabolism. She still ran every day, but never in the morning.

"The men don't really want to date me. They just like the attention I pay them. They tend to forget they are paying *me* to pay attention. And I know far too much about them too soon."

An alert on her tablet told her she'd received a new email. Jan pushed herself to her feet. "I'll let you get back to work. Do you want another cup of coffee?"

Brodie already had caffeine-filled veins but why should that matter? "Please."

She swiped her finger across her tablet and accessed her inbox. She'd received quite a few messages when she'd been dealing with Mr. Suave but only one made her pulse accelerate.

Your donation to the auction at the Mavericks' Charity Ball filled the subject line and all the moisture in her mouth disappeared. Jeez, she'd had a brief encounter with Kade months ago, shouldn't she have forgotten about him by now?

Unfortunately Kade wasn't the type of man who was easily forgotten. And, if she had to be truthful, she still missed those early-morning runs when it seemed like they had the park to themselves. She missed the way her heart kicked up when she saw him, missed the way he pushed her to run faster, train harder. She'd enjoyed him, enjoyed that time with him, more than she should have.

Brodie rubbed her hands over her face and gave herself a mental slap. She was almost thirty, a successful business owner and matchmaker to some of the sharpest, richest, most successful bachelors in the city. She should not be thinking about *the* sharpest, richest, best-looking bachelor in the city.

Pathetic squared. Brodie shook her head at her ridiculousness and opened the email.

Dear Ms. Stewart,
On behalf of the Chief Executive Officer of the Vancouver Mavericks, Kade Webb, may I extend our heartfelt gratitude for your donation to the Mavericks' auction to be held on June 19.

Attached is your invitation to a luncheon my department is hosting for our valued sponsors earlier on the day. You are most welcome to attend the ball and charity auction; the cost and details are attached.

We look forward to your presence at lunch on the 19 of June. Please see the attached document for the venue and time.
Yours,
Wren Bayliss
Public Relations Director
Vancouver Mavericks

Thanks but, no thanks. She wouldn't be attending. Donating to the charity auction had been Colin's idea and he could attend the luncheon and ball on their behalf. She wasn't even sure donating their services to the charity auction would raise any money… What bachelor or bachelorette would admit to wanting to use a matchmaker in a room full of their friends and colleagues? Their business was based on discretion and her clients came to her, mostly, via word of mouth. But Wren, and Colin, had dismissed Brodie's concerns. They seemed to think sisters, brothers and friends would bid on their siblings' or friends' behalf. Besides, the guest could bid silently via cell phone as well, so anonymity, if it was required, would be assured.

Thanks to the competition of online matchmaking Colin was convinced they needed to cement their position as matchmakers to the elite of Vancouver society and they needed to network more and foster relationships. Being part of the Mavericks' silent auction was a huge coup and would be excellent direct advertising to their target group. Since marketing and PR was Colin's forte, she'd told him he could represent them at the luncheon.

Yes, a part of her reluctance was the fact there was a chance Kade would be at the function. Months might've passed but she was still embarrassed down to her two-inch designer heels. She'd acted like a ditzy virgin who said yes but meant no. God! How could she be in the same room with him without wanting to jump him—the man still fueled her sexual fantasies—but also wanting to hide under the table?

Her computer dinged again and she looked at the new message that popped into her inbox.

Hey, Brodes,
I presume you received an invite to attend the sponsor's lunch hosted by the Mavericks? I can't attend. Kay and I are seeing a fertility specialist that day. Can you go and do the thing for us both?
Thanks,
Col

Brodie groaned.

Please let Kade not be there, she prayed.

Two

"Whose stupid idea was this?"

Kade Webb scowled at his two best friends and rolled his shoulders under his suit jacket, wishing he was anywhere but in the crowded, over-perfumed bar area of Taste, one of the best restaurants in Vancouver. He'd spent most of last night reading P&L statements and had spent a long, tedious morning with Josh Logan's hard-ass agent negotiating a deal to buy the hotshot wing, and all he wanted was to plant himself behind his messy desk and make a dent in his paperwork. He was trying to finalize their—his, Mac's and Quinn's—partnership with old man Bayliss, Wren's grandfather, so the four of them could make a solid counteroffer to buy the Mavericks franchise before Vernon's widow sold it to Boris Chenko, a Russian billionaire who owned a string of now generic sports franchises.

Kade didn't have the time to socialize. To play nice.

What he really wanted, despite it only being noon, was a cold beer, a long shower and some hot sex. Or, to save time, some long, hot sex in a shower. Since he hadn't had time to date lately the hot sex would have to be a solo act later—how sad, too bad—but really, he'd give it all up, sex included, for a solid eight hours of sleep.

He was burning the candle at both ends and somewhere in the middle, as well.

"Will you please take that scowl off your face?"

Kade looked down into the face of his newly appointed director of public relations and wondered, for the hundredth time, why there was no sexual attraction between him and Wren. She was gorgeous, slim, vivacious and smart, but she didn't rock his boat. He didn't rock hers, either. They were friends, just like he was with Mac's new fiancée, Rory, and for the first time in Kade's life he was enjoying uncomplicated female relationships.

That being said, he still wouldn't say no to some uncomplicated sex.

"Kade, concentrate!" Wren slammed her elbow into his side and he pulled his attention back to business.

"Your guests of honor, the main sponsors, should

be arriving any minute and you need to pay them some special attention," Wren insisted, a tiny foot tapping her only indication of nervousness.

"Who are they again?"

Frustration flashed in Wren's blue eyes and Kade held up his hands in apology. "Wren, I've been dealing with player negotiations and your grandfather as our new partner, and fending off Myra's demands for us to make a counteroffer. Sponsors for this ball haven't been high on my priority list."

"Did you read *any* of the memos I sent you?"

Kade shrugged. "Sorry, no. But you can tell me now and I'll remember."

He had a phenomenal memory. It was a skill he acquired as a child hopping from town to town and school to school following the whims of his artist father. Within a day of arriving in a new place, he'd find a map and memorize the street names so he'd know exactly where he was at all times. He'd felt emotionally lost so often that being physically lost was going a step too far. His memory helped him catch up with schoolwork and remember the names of teachers and potential friends, so he could ease his way through another set of new experiences.

Wren ran through the list of the bigger donations and then said, "The Forde Gallery donated one of your father's paintings, a small watercolor but pretty."

Jeez, he remembered when his father had to swap paintings for food or gas or rent money. Even his small paintings now went for ten grand or more… It was a hell of a donation.

"We have dinners on yachts, holidays, jewelry, the usual bits and pieces businesses donate. The item that will be the most fun and will get the crowd buzzing is the matchmaking service…"

"The what?"

"Brodie Stewart and Colin Jones are providing their matchmaking services. The winners, one girl and one guy, will be matched up and sent on three dates to find a potential mate. Sounds like fun, doesn't it?"

Brodie Stewart? His Brodie? The girl who'd kissed like a dream but who'd bailed on him before they got to the bedroom?

"It sounds like hell." Kade managed to utter the response even though his mind was filled with memories of Brodie, dark hair spilling over her shoulders as she lay against his chest, bright green eyes languid and dreamy after one spectacular hot, wet kiss. He dimly recalled her saying something about her having her own business but why did he think she was in consulting?

"Is she attending this lunch?" Kade asked and hoped Wren, or his friends, didn't hear the note of excitement in his voice.

"You know this Brodie person?" Quinn demanded. And there was the problem with being friends with someone for so damn long. There was little you could get past them.

"Not really," Kade replied, sounding bored.

"Let me give you a hint about your boss, Wren," Mac stated, his arm around Rory's waist. "When he lies he always sounds disinterested, faraway, detached."

Unfortunately, being in love hadn't affected Mac's observational skills and he was as sharp as ever. "Shut the hell up, McCaskill, you have no idea what you are talking about. I met Brodie once, a while ago."

"Why didn't you tell us about her?" Quinn demanded, unsatisfied.

"Do you tell me about the women you meet?" Kade responded.

Quinn thought for a moment before grinning. "Pretty much, yeah. And if I don't tell you, then the press will."

Kade pulled a face. The society pages of their local papers and many internet sites devoted far too much time speculating about their love lives. Mac had provided a break for Kade and Quinn as the media devoured the news that he was settling down with the lovely Rory, but recently they'd restarted their probing inquiries about the state of his and Quinn's love lives. Many of the papers hinted, or outright demanded, it was time the other two "Maverick-teers" followed Mac's example.

Kade felt that he would rather kiss an Amazonian dart frog.

Only Mac and Quinn knew his past, knew about

his unconventional upbringing as the son of a mostly itinerant artist who dragged him from place to place and town to town on a whim. They understood his need to feel financially secure and because they worked together, invested together and always stuck together, the three of them, along with Wren's grandfather, were in the position to buy their beloved hockey team, the Vancouver Mavericks.

Yeah, he might be, along with Quinn, a wealthy, eligible and elusive bachelor, but he had every intention of staying that way. Legalities and partnership agreements and a million miles of red tape—and his belief in the loyalty of his friends—had allowed him to commit to his career with the Mavericks, formerly as a player and now as the CEO and, hopefully, as a future co-owner. But a personal commitment? Hell no.

He'd learned that hard lesson as a child. As soon as he found someone to love—a dog, a friend, a teacher, a coach—his father would rip it away by packing up their lives and moving them along. Emotional involvement sent Kade backward to his powerless childhood.

He'd hated that feeling then and he loathed it now. His theory was if you didn't play in a rainstorm, then you wouldn't get hit by lightning. He made damn sure the women he dated had no expectations, that they thoroughly understood he was a here-now-gone-tomorrow type of guy. That they shouldn't expect anything from him.

Despite his up-front attitude, there were always women who thought they could change his mind so he'd still had to ease himself out of situations. Sometimes he managed it with charm, sometimes he had to be blunt, but when he sensed his lovers were becoming emotionally invested, he backed off. Way, way off.

Brodie Stewart was the only woman who'd ever turned the tables on him, who'd backed away before he could. Backed away before he'd even gotten her into bed.

"...she had all the emotional depth of a puddle!"

Kade pulled his attention back to the conversation and caught the tail end of Rory's comment. She was scowling at Quinn and he looked unrepentant, being his bad-boy self.

"Honey, I wasn't dating her for her conversational skills," Quinn stated.

Rory shook her head and rested her chin on Mac's shoulder. "One day you are going to meet someone who you can't resist and I hope she gives you hell," Rory said, her tone and expression fierce.

"Rorks, unfortunately butt-face here claimed you before I did so I am destined to be a free spirit." Quinn put his hand on his heart, his eyes laughing.

Rory, smart girl that she was, didn't fall for Quinn's BS. Instead, she poked Quinn's stomach. "You will meet her and I will not only laugh while I watch you run around her like a headless chicken, I will encourage her to give you as much trouble as possible." She stretched past Quinn to jab Kade in the stomach. "That goes for you, too, Kade. The female population of Vancouver has spoiled you two rotten."

"I'm not complaining." Kade smiled, taking a sip of his lime-flavored water.

"Me neither," Quinn quickly agreed. He stuck his tongue in his cheek as he continued to tease Rory. "And I don't think we've been spoiled—we've been treated as per our elevated status as hockey gods."

"That just shows how moronic some women can be," Rory muttered. She looked up at Mac and narrowed her eyes. "You're very quiet, McCaskill. Got anything to say?"

Mac dropped a kiss on her forehead and another on her mouth. "Hell no! This is your argument with my friends. But, since I am taking you home and hoping to get lucky, I'll just agree with everything you say."

Quinn made the sound of a cracking whip and Kade rolled his eyes before he said, "Wimp."

"You might wear the trousers but Rory picks them out," Quinn added and immediately stepped back to lessen the impact of Mac's big fist smacking his shoulder. "May I point out that before Rory snagged you, you were—"

"No, you absolutely may not." Wren's cool voice interrupted their smack talk. "Can you three please act like the responsible, smart businessmen that people—mistakenly I might add—think you are and behave yourselves? The first sponsor has arrived."

Kade didn't need Wren's nod toward the ballroom to tell him Brodie had arrived. He'd felt the prickle of anticipation between his shoulder blades, felt the energy in the room change. He was super aware of her. As he slowly turned, he felt the world fade away.

She hadn't changed, yet…she had. It had only been six months, but somehow she was a great deal more attractive than he remembered. Her dress hugged a toned body and her long black hair was now a short, feathery cap against her head. What definitely hadn't changed was her ability to send all his blood rocketing south to a very obvious and inconvenient place.

"Well, well, well…isn't this interesting?" Mac drawled in Kade's ear.

"First time I've seen our boy gobsmacked, dude," Quinn added. "Shut your mouth, boyo, you're drooling."

Kade ignored his friends. Life had unexpectedly dropped Brodie back into his realm again and he wanted what he'd always wanted every time he'd laid eyes on her: Brodie in his bed, under him, naked and legs around him…eyes begging for him to come on in.

Her perfume reached him before she did and he realized it was the same scent he remembered. It took him straight back to those early-morning runs in the park, to crisp air and the hesitant smile of the black-haired girl who waited for him by the running store and kept up with his fast pace along the seawall. He hadn't run in the park since the morning he'd heard about Vernon's death.

And kissed Brodie.

It had been an incredible kiss and the one highlight of a couple of really tough, horrible months. If only he had the memory of taking her to bed, too…

So it turned out he didn't want long, hot sex with any random woman. He wanted to make love to Brodie. Interesting.

Crazy.

And pretty damn dangerous. He wouldn't—couldn't—allow her to know the effect she had on him, how he instantly craved her and the crazy chemical reaction he was experiencing. It wasn't clever to admit she was the only woman he'd ever encountered who could thoroughly disconcert him, who could wipe every rational thought from his brain.

Okay, he was officially losing it. Maybe it was time, as Wren had suggested, he started acting like the CEO he was supposed to be.

With anyone else, he could do it with his eyes closed. Around Brodie, he might have to put his back into it.

So here goes…

Brodie held out her hand to Kade and hoped her smile wasn't as shaky as she felt. "Kade, it's been a while."

"Brodie." Kade took her hand and she held his eyes even though her pulse skittered up her arm and straight to her belly. She met his eyes and felt her heart roll over, as it always did. She knew his eyes were a deep brown but today, against his olive complexion and dark blond hair, they glinted black.

Oh, this wasn't good. He was a sexy man. They'd kissed but that wasn't enough of a reason for her hormones to start doing their crazy dance. She looked down at their intertwined hands and could easily remember what his tanned fingers felt like on her back, his wide hand sliding over her butt, his lips on hers...

Dammit, Brodie!

Kade touched her elbow and gestured to his friends. Hot, hot and *steamin'*. Brodie wanted to fan herself. Quinn Rayne was the ultimate sexy bad boy, Mac McCaskill was even better looking—if that was possible—after falling in love with the attractive woman tucked into his side, and Kade...? Why, with him looking as fantastic as he did, the urge to jump him and do him on the nearest table was nearly overwhelming.

This was the problem with Kade Webb, Brodie reminded herself. He had the ability to turn her from a woman who considered all the angles into a wild child who acted first and regretted later. She hadn't made an impulsive decision for nearly a decade and yet, around him, that was all she seemed to do! For weeks she'd met him in the park as the sun rose. Then she'd accompanied him home, kissed him senseless and been so tempted to make love to him. Around him, *impulsive* was her new middle name.

Stewart, start acting like the adult you are! Immediately!

Pulling herself together, Brodie greeted Kade's friends, kissed Wren hello and looked, and sounded, like the professional she normally was.

Quinn smiled at her. Whoo boy, it was a potent grin and she could easily imagine girls falling like flies at his feet. That smile should be registered as a weapon of mass destruction, but Brodie caught the wariness in his eyes and the intelligence he hid behind his charm. "So, you're Brodie."

"I am."

"And you're a matchmaker."

"I am." Brodie tipped her head, assessing him. "Would you like me to find you someone?"

She had to smile when Quinn flushed and sent a help-me look at his friends. Since Quinn's exploits, mostly in love, kept Vancouver entertained on a weekly basis, she knew he had no problem finding a date. Finding a *partner* was a very different story.

"You know, most of my clients don't have any problems meeting women and they often date a variety of women."

Quinn frowned. "So why do they need you?"

"Because they are dating the wrong type of women. They want to be in a relationship," Brodie patiently explained. "Do you want to be in a relationship, Mr. Rayne?"

She was taking the circuitous route to find out what she desperately wanted to know: would Kade be bidding for her matchmaking services? The thought of matching him to any of Colin's clients made her stomach roil. Colin's clients were wonderful women, but Brodie thought the *ick* factor was a bit too high to match her fantasy man with a flesh-and-bone woman.

She'd rather pick her eyes out with a cake fork.

"Hell no! And why am I the focus of attention?" Quinn complained. "Kade is as much of a lone wolf as me!"

Brodie lifted an eyebrow in Kade's direction, as if to say "Are you?" He immediately read her question and responded with an inscrutable smile.

Brodie looked around, her eyes falling on the honey blonde surgically attached to Mac's side. Rory's look was speculative, bouncing from Quinn to Kade and back again. Brodie recognized her assessing, mischievous look. This was a woman wanting to cause trouble…

Mac's deep voice broke her train of thought. "Your hands are empty, Brodie. What would you like to drink? Wine? A soda?"

A small glass of wine couldn't hurt, could it? "I'd love a glass of Tangled Vine Chardonnay."

Rory tipped her head and looked at Quinn. "Is that the wine you brought over the other night? It was seriously yummy."

Quinn nodded. "I'll bring a case over tonight. What's for supper?"

"Risotto. Troy is joining us tonight," Rory replied.

Mac looked appalled. "We're having them for supper again? Troy I don't mind, but these two? Babe, they are like rats, if you keep feeding them, we are never going to get rid of them."

"Kade and I are the rats," Quinn told Brodie, smiling. He lifted a huge shoulder. "What can I say? She's a good cook."

Brodie looked into Mac's eyes and noticed the amusement under his fake scowl. Yeah, he looked hard-ass and a bit scary—they all did—but she could see these men shared a bond that went beyond love. It was too easy to say they loved each other, but it was more than that; there was loyalty here and support, a deep and profound desire to make sure their "brothers" were happy. She couldn't help feeling envious of their bond despite knowing she'd chosen her solitary state. She'd had friendships like that; bonds with Jay and Chels that couldn't be broken by anything except death.

She still missed them, every day. She missed the people who could finish her sentences, who got her jokes. She missed the I-know-it's-after-midnight-but-I-brought-you-pizza conversations. She missed Chelsea, missed those crazy antics—"I'm outside your window and I have a date. Toss down your lucky belt/new shoes/red lipstick/flirty dress."

She missed Jay, the boy who knew her inside out, the man she'd just been getting to know. His sweet kisses, his endless support, his newly acquired fascination with her body. She still missed the man she thought she'd spend the rest of her life with…

She hadn't been able to reconnect with people on that level again. She wasn't prepared to risk heartbreak. Having her heart dented by loss and being left behind without any emotional support sucked. It stung. It burned. It made her cautious and wary. Scared.

She was very okay with being scared. "And I'm sending you a bill for the food we buy," Mac grumbled. "Spongers."

"Rory's a great cook and she likes having us around. Maybe she needs a break from you," Quinn told Mac as he took the glass of wine Kade had ordered for her off the waiter's tray and handed it to Brodie, ignoring Kade's scowl. "I'll bring the wine."

Rory grinned. "Excellent. I love that wine."

"Might I remind you that you won't be able to drink it for a year or so?" Mac muttered.

Rory frowned and then her expression cleared and a small, tender smile drifted across her face. She touched her stomach and Brodie immediately caught on. It took Mac's friends seconds longer to catch up. And, judging by Quinn's and Kade's stunned faces, that wasn't news they'd been expecting. But once they realized what Mac had revealed, they swept Rory into their arms for a long, emotional hug. Kade hugged Mac, as did Quinn, and Brodie felt tears prick her eyes at their joy for their friend. She stepped back, feeling she shouldn't be here, sharing this precious, intimate moment. She half smiled when she noticed Wren doing the same thing.

Weird that Brodie seemed to be present for some of the big, personal Maverick moments. Vernon's death, Mac's baby… She was an outsider, on the wrong side of this magical circle, so it didn't make sense that she was again in the position to hear something deeply personal. This time, at least, it was good news.

"This wasn't how we planned on telling you," Rory said, jamming her elbow into Mac's side.

Brodie looked at Rory, who had her back to Mac's chest, his big hands on her still very flat stomach. "Congratulations," she murmured.

"Yeah, huge congratulations," Kade said, before slanting a sly look at Mac. "Now you're going to have two children under your feet, Rorks."

"Ha-ha." Mac scowled.

"I know, right?" Rory replied, her voice wobbly. "I'm going to be a mommy, Kade."

"You'll be great at it," Kade assured her and tipped his head at Mac. "But he'll need some training."

"I'm not old enough to have friends who are about to be parents." Quinn clapped Mac on the shoulder and nodded to the bar. "We definitely need champagne. I'll get some."

Wren shook her head and stepped forward. "As much as I hate to break up the party we have work to do and a lunch to host."

Quinn wrinkled his nose. "Our head girl has spoken."

Wren threaded a hand through his arm and pulled him toward the dining area. "C'mon, brat. I've put you at a table where you can't misbehave."

Brodie felt Kade's hand on her back and she immediately, subconsciously moved closer to him, her fingers accidentally brushing the outside of his hard thigh.

Kade tipped his head and dropped his voice so only she could hear his words. "It hasn't gone away, has it?"

Brodie wished she could deny it, dismiss his comment, but she couldn't lie to him. Or herself. She forced herself to look him in the eye. "No."

His fingers pushed into her back at her reluctant admission. "So, just to be clear, we're saying this crazy attraction is still happening?"

"Yep." One-syllable answers were all she could manage.

"So are we going to do anything about it this time?"

Wren's efficient voice interrupted their low, intense conversation. "Kade, you're at the main table up front. Brodie, I'll show you to your seat."

Brodie gave Kade a little shrug and followed Wren into the private dining room of Taste. When she tossed a look over her shoulder, she flushed when she noticed Kade was still watching her.

And he didn't stop looking at her for the next ninety minutes.

* * *

He wanted her. The heated looks they'd exchanged over the three tables that separated them left her in no doubt of that. Jeez, it was a minor miracle the room hadn't spontaneously combusted from the sparks they were throwing at each other.

He wanted her as much as he had six months ago, possibly more. It was insane; it was exciting.

What *was* she going to do about it?

She knew what he wanted, to take up where they'd left off in his loft. In the ladies' room Brodie pulled a face at her reflection in the mirror above the bathroom sink and ran her wet fingers over the back of her neck, hoping to cool herself down but knowing it was a futile gesture. She was hot from the inside out and it was all Kade Webb's fault.

Every look he'd sent her, every small smile, had told her he wanted her in the most basic, biblical way possible.

She was pretty sure she'd returned his message. With interest.

Brodie sighed. Having a fling with Kade wouldn't hurt anyone. Unlike an affair with a married man it wasn't icky, immoral or dishonest. It wouldn't be embarrassing or hurtful. It wouldn't—unless she did something really stupid, like fall for the guy—be painful.

She hadn't had an affair, or sex, for a long, long time; she hadn't been naked with a man since Jared the IT guy and he was around three, or was it four, years ago? She was nearly thirty and she was tired of dating herself.

Could she do it? Could she have a one-night stand with Kade? Was she okay with being another puck he shot into his sexual net? Brodie grimaced at her bad analogy. But could she be another of Webb's Women?

If she was looking for a relationship, and she wasn't because she was relationship-phobic, Kade would be the last person she'd be interested in. Brodie gripped the vanity and stared at the basin, thinking hard.

He was famous and she'd matched enough semi-famous guys to know how much time and effort it took to date a celebrity. She couldn't think of anything worse than having your life dissected on social media platforms or in the society columns, but some women got off on it.

She hadn't considered any of this that long-ago morning when she'd agreed to coffee. Everything had moved so quickly and she'd only been thinking in terms of a couple of hours spent with him. But she had noticed that over the last six months the spotlight on Kade had become even bigger and brighter. His life was routinely dissected; his dates scrutinized. The press was relentless and easily turned a movie into a marriage proposal, a dinner into destiny.

Brodie shuddered. Yuck.

That being said, she still wanted him.

If she could go through with it this time—and that was a big if—she couldn't ignore the fact that a quick fling with Vancouver's most eligible, slippery bachelor could have consequences. If they did do the deed and it became public knowledge, as these things tended to do with the Mavericks, it would affect her business. She had a database of clients who trusted her, who confided in her. Quite a few of them thought she was engaged, and a liaison with Kade would not inspire her clients to trust her judgment.

Men, she'd realized, were frequently a lot more romantic—or traditional—than most woman gave them credit for. They could have affairs, play the field and have one-night stands, but they wouldn't appreciate their matchmaker doing the same.

No, it was smarter and so much more sensible to ignore Kade's suggestion that they continue what they'd started. Sleeping with him probably wouldn't be as good as she imagined; she'd probably romanticized exactly how good Webb's kissing was to excuse her crazy, uninhibited behaviour when she was alone with him. No, best to keep her distance…

Good decision, Brodie thought, eyeing her reflection in the mirror. Sensible decision.

Adult decision.

Safe decision.

So why did it feel so damn *wrong*?

Three

The ladies' room was on a short flight of stairs above the men's restroom and when she stepped into the passage, she looked down and saw the blond head and muscular shoulders that could only belong to Kade.

She flicked off a piece of fluff from her shocking pink blouson dress, belted at the waist and ending midthigh. Nude heels, scalpel-thin, made her legs look like they went on for miles. Back in her apartment it had seemed very suitable for a business lunch, but when Kade looked up and his eyes darkened from a deep brown to a shade just off black, she knew he wanted to rip off her clothing with his teeth. Keeping her hand on the banister, biting the inside of her lip, her heart galloping, she walked down the three steps to the marble floor, a scant couple of inches from his broad chest.

He didn't give her any warning or ask for her permission, his mouth simply slammed into hers. Brodie had to grab his biceps to keep from falling off her shoes. Those amazing hands covered a great deal of her back and she was sure her dress would sport scorch marks from the heat. She was intensely aware of him and could feel the ridges of his fingers, the strength in his wrists.

Brodie wound her arms around his neck and pressed her mouth against his. He tasted like coffee and Kade and breath mints and his lips seemed to feel like old friends. Warm, firm, dry. Confident. That word again. His hands bumped up her spine, kneading as he worked his way to her shoulders, moving around to catch her face. His thumbs skated over her cheekbones as he deepened the kiss, his tongue sliding into her mouth.

Loneliness—the slight dissatisfaction that hovered like a fine mist around her, the ever-present sorrow—dissipated as he took command of the kiss, pushing her back against the wall and pushing his knee between her thighs. This was kissing—raw, raunchy, flat-out sexy. Brodie felt heat and warmth and moisture gather and felt an unfamiliar pull of fulfillment, a desire to lose herself in the heat and strength and sexiness of this man.

Kade's hand skimmed the side of her chest, down

her waist and around to her butt, his fingers strong and sure, experienced. He cupped a cheek, pulled her up and into him, and she sighed as his erection pushed into her stomach. He yanked his mouth off hers and she tumbled into his sinfully dark eyes. "Same old, same old."

Brodie placed her hands on his pecs and tried to regulate her breathing. Where was an oxygen tank when she needed one? She felt Kade's fingers on her cheekbone, tracing her jaw. "Brodie? You okay?"

Fine. Just trying to get my brain to restart. Brodie placed her forehead on his sternum and pulled in some much needed air.

"Dammit, Kade," she eventually muttered.

"Yep, we're a fire hazard," Kade agreed, resting his chin on the top of her head. "What are we going to do about it?"

"Nothing?" Brodie suggested.

"Yeah…not an option." She heard the determination in his voice. She knew he would do what it took to get what he wanted.

What *she* wanted. He wouldn't need to do much persuading—she was halfway to following him to hell and back for an orgasm or two.

She was allowed to share some amazing sex with someone who knew what he was doing, her usually quiet wild child insisted. She was twenty-nine, mostly normal but terribly sexually frustrated.

You had this argument with yourself earlier. He's

single. You're single. You don't need anyone's permission...

Kade didn't need to use charm, or to say anything at all. She was doing a fine job of talking herself into his bed all on her own.

"Brodie?" Kade stepped back and bent his knees so he could look her in the eye. "What do you say? Do you want to take this to its very natural conclusion?"

Brodie gripped his big biceps, or as much of it as she could get into her hand. He felt harder, more muscular than she remembered. How was that possible? She wanted to undo the buttons on his shirt, push aside the fabric and see what other wonders lay under his expensive clothes. Was his chest bigger? His shoulders broader? His thighs stronger?

"Are you going to put me out of my misery sometime soon?" Kade asked. He sounded like sleeping with her was neither here nor there. Then she took another look at his expression, read the emotion in his eyes.

There was frustration, a whole lot of desire and a hint of panic. Because he thought she might say no? He looked a little off-kilter and not as suave and as confident as she'd first suspected. His hint of insecurity made her feel steadier. That their chemistry had rocked him allowed her to regain her mental and emotional balance.

"God, woman, you're killing me."

She knew if she said yes, there would be no going

back. She couldn't get cold feet, couldn't retreat this time.

She was a little scared—and she should be. She'd laid out all the arguments in the ladies' room. But she could no more stop a freight train than miss this second chance to find out if he was as good as her imagination insisted.

Time to put them both out of their misery. Brodie slowly nodded. "Yeah, let's revisit the past. One night, not a big deal?"

"You sure?"

She knew he was asking for some reassurance she wouldn't change her mind midway through, so she placed her hand on his cheek and nodded. "Very sure. On the understanding this is a one-time thing and it stays between us."

Relief flashed across Kade's face and she felt his fingers flexing on her back. "I never kiss and tell. But are you sure we'll be able to stop after one night?"

Brodie shrugged. Probably not. "We can give it our best shot."

Kade stepped back and ran a hand around the back of his neck. "Interesting," he said.

Brodie frowned. "What is?"

"You have a very…businesslike approach to life. And sex."

She supposed she did, but life had taught her to put emotion away from daily life. If she allowed emotion to rule, she would've crawled into a cave after the accident and never come out. She turned her back on her feelings because they were so big, so overwhelming. Before the tragedy, she'd loved hard… wildly, uninhibitedly. She'd engaged every one of her senses and she'd been the most emotional creature imaginable.

A car accident had taken her family, but emotion had hung around and nearly killed her, too. To survive she'd had to box it up and push it away…because she couldn't feel happy without feeling sad. No joy without pain. No love without heartbreak.

It was easier just to skate.

Brodie lifted her chin and sent Kade a cool smile. Time to get the conversation back on track. "So, when and where?"

Kade lifted his eyebrows in surprise and Brodie sent him a look, daring him to make another comment about her frankness. He looked like he wanted to and Brodie prayed he wouldn't. Kade seemed to have the ability to look beyond her shell to the mess inside…

She didn't need anyone upsetting her mental apple cart.

Kade looked at his watch and thought for a minute. "I have meetings this afternoon or else I'd whisk you back to my place right now."

That was something her old self would've done, Brodie mused. Breakfast at midnight, dancing in the rain, unplanned road trips and afternoon sex. The Brodie she was today didn't do wild anymore.

"And tonight is the ball. Are you coming?" Kade placed his hand flat on the wall behind her head and she had to resist the urge to rest her temple on his forearm.

Brodie shook her head. "No. Besides the tickets are sold out."

The corners of Kade's mouth tipped up. "I'm sure I know someone who can slip you inside."

It was tempting, Brodie thought, but no. Attending the ball with Kade would make it seem like a date and she didn't *date*.

"Why don't you give me a call in a day or two?" she suggested.

"I don't know if I can last that long," Kade said, his tone rueful. He jammed his hands into his suit pockets and Brodie couldn't help her urge to straighten his tie. "But...okay."

"Lipstick on my face?" he asked.

"No, you're fine."

Kade nodded. "Give me your cell number. And your address."

Brodie put the info in his phone. Kade nodded his thanks.

Kade's eyes warmed to the color of rough cocoa. "Do you work from home?"

"No, I share an office with my friend and associate downtown. He's also a matchmaker."

Kade scratched his chin. "I am still wrapping my head around the fact you set people up and they pay you for it. It's...weird."

She couldn't take offense. Frequently she thought it was a very odd way to earn money—especially for someone who'd once specialized in international banking and who intended to remain single for the rest of her life. But she was curious as to why he thought her business was weird so she asked him.

Kade rubbed the back of his neck. "I guess it's because I've never had a problem finding dates.'

It was such a common misconception. "Neither do most of my clients. They aren't looking to date, they are looking to settle down." She saw him wince and she had to smile. "So I guess you're not going to be a client anytime soon?"

"Or ever."

Kade pushed all thoughts of her career out of her head when he lifted his hands to cradle her face. She shivered with a mixture of lust and longing. Her hands drifted across his chest and skimmed his flat, ridged belly.

"I can't wait to spend some time with you." He bent to kiss the sensitive spot between her shoulder and neck. He lifted his head and gave her a hard stare. "Soon, I promise."

Brodie swallowed in an attempt to put some saliva back into her mouth.

Keeping his hands on her face, Kade twisted his wrist to check the time and softly cursed. "I've got to get back to the office, I am so late." The pad of his thumb brushed her bottom lip. "Please don't talk yourself out of this, Brodie."

She wanted to protest, wanted to reassure him, but she didn't. "See you."

Kade nodded abruptly, dropped a hard, open-mouthed kiss on her lips, then whipped around and headed back to the restaurant.

"You'd better make it very soon, Kade Webb."

She'd run ten kilometers and had a cold shower, and despite it being four hours later, she could still taste Kade on her lips. Her lady parts were buzzing; her heart was still thumping. Her heart rate had actually *dropped* when she'd all but sprinted around Stanley Park. How was she going to function for the next couple of days if this heightened state of awareness didn't dissipate?

It had to dissipate—she couldn't live like this.

God, this was why she ran from entanglements. It was so much easier to slide on the surface of life. She didn't like feeling this way. It felt too much like she was…

Well, *living.* Living meant anticipation, excitement, lust, passion. She wasn't good at any of it anymore and she didn't deserve to feel all that, not when her entire family, practically everyone she had ever loved, was no longer around to do the same.

Why didn't I get hurt?

Why did I live when other people died?

Survivor's guilt. She was the poster child for the condition. Brodie walked across her living room, hands on her hips, her brow furrowed. She'd seen the psychologists, read the literature. She knew guilt was common and part of the healing process. Her healing process was taking a damn long time. She knew she isolated herself. Living a half life wasn't healthy—it certainly couldn't bring her loved ones back. But she couldn't stop thinking she didn't deserve to be happy.

Love was impossible.

The sound of her intercom buzzing broke into her thoughts. Brodie pushed back her hair, frowning. She wasn't expecting anybody—her great-aunt Poppy, who lived on the floor below, was out of town—so she couldn't imagine who could be leaning on her doorbell.

Brodie walked to her front door and pressed the switch. "Can I help you?"

"I have ninety minutes, can I come up?"

Kade. Holy freakin'… Because her mouth was instantly bone-dry, she found it difficult to form words.

"C'mon, babe, don't make me beg," Kade cajoled.

This was madness. This was crazy. She should tell him to leave, tell him that she didn't want him to come up. But that would be a big, fat lie… She did want to see him, preferably naked.

So Brodie pressed the button to open the door downstairs and wrenched open her apartment door to watch him run up. He was still dressed in his suit from earlier. His tie was pulled down and he carried a small gym bag and a tuxedo covered in plastic over his shoulder.

Hunky, sexy, determined man, Brodie thought, leaning against the door frame. Kade reached her and flashed a quick smile but didn't say a word. He just grabbed her hand, yanked her inside, kicked her door closed and threw his stuff on the nearest chair. Then two strong hands gripped her hips and swept her up and into him, her feet leaving the floor. Then his mouth was on hers, warm and demanding, and his tongue swept inside, allowing her to taste his frustration-coated passion.

Whoo-boy!

After a minute had passed—or a millennium, who could tell?—Kade gently lowered Brodie to her feet, but he kept his lips on hers, his tongue delving and dancing. She responded, awed by the pent-up longing she felt in the intensity of his kiss. Her response must have seemed just as demanding, as urgent. Brodie moved her hands to his shirt, tugging it out of his pants. Desperate to feel his skin on hers, she moaned her frustration and then resented the brief separation from Kade's body as he stepped away to unbutton and remove his shirt.

Brodie moved forward and ran her lips across his bare chest, stopping to flicker her tongue over his nipple, to rub her cheek on his chest hair. He was such a man. From the hardness of his muscles to the slightly rough texture of his skin and the smell that called to her senses, he awakened every cell in her body. She could no more stop this than she could stop a freight train. Neither did she want to, she realized.

She needed him, right now. She had to have him—in her, around her, sharing this with her.

"Bed," Kade muttered against her jawline.

"Too far." Brodie managed to lift a hand and wave to the right. "Desk, over there."

"That'll work."

Running his hands over her bottom, Kade lifted Brodie onto the edge of the desk and pushed the files and papers off the table. They slid and tumbled to the floor. She didn't care. Part of her knew this was a mistake, but she didn't care about that, either. Nothing mattered but having him in her arms, allowing him to make indescribably delicious love to her.

Kade quickly stripped her of her clothing, while Brodie watched him through heavy, half-closed eyes. Keeping one hand on her breast, he reached into his suit pants and yanked his wallet out of a pocket. Scattering cards and cash, he found a condom and ripped it open with his teeth. He shed the rest of his clothes, and slipped the condom on. Brodie was not shocked when Kade grabbed the flimsy material of her panties and ripped them off her. His erection was hard and proud as he rubbed himself against her most secret places, seeking her permission to enter.

His lips followed his erection, and Brodie thought she would turn to liquid. Just when she could tolerate no more, Kade lifted his head to worship her breasts with his mouth, tongue and lips. Brodie closed her fingers around him and relished the sound of his breathing, heavy in the quiet of the early evening.

Brown eyes met green as she tugged him toward her. Kade's one hand slid under her hip and the other cradled her head, both encouraging her to ride with him.

The desk felt like a soft bed. The cold coffee she'd left there earlier could have been the finest champagne, the mixed-up papers rose petals. They were locked together. Finally. Kade moved within her and Brodie followed. Kade demanded and she replied. Deeper, longer, higher, faster. She met him stroke for stroke, matching his passion, uninhibited, free.

On that thought Brodie fractured on a yell and a sob. Then Kade bucked and arched and collapsed against her, his body hot.

"Brodie?" he muttered against her shoulder. "You alive?"

"Uh-huh."

"Desk survived?"

Brodie's mouth curved into a smile. She patted the wood next to her hip. "Looks like it. You?"

Kade kissed her neck before reluctantly pulling out of her. He straightened and turned away. "Yeah, I'm fine—"

Brodie sat up and frowned at his stream of curses. "What on earth…?"

Kade grimaced at the condom in his hand and then back to her. "The condom split. Dammit, it was brand-new."

Brodie hopped down from the desk and looked around for her shirt, which had landed on the back of her couch. Well, that was a big bucket of freezing water. Dressing quickly, she thought about what to say, how to act. Expressing anger or disappointment was sort of like bolting the stable door after the horse had fled. It wouldn't help. So she decided to be practical.

"If you want to, uh…clean up, my bedroom has an en suite bathroom, second door on the right."

Kade, utterly unconcerned with his nudity, stalked away. Brodie folded his suit pants, hung his shirt over the back of a chair and tucked his socks into his shoes. Picking up her ruined panties, she balled them in her hands before walking into her kitchen and throwing them into the trash can.

Putting her hands on her hips, she considered the angles. What were the chances of her becoming pregnant? She was on a contraceptive, which she took religiously. Was it even the right time of the month for her to be ovulating? Walking toward the calendar she kept on the side of her fridge, she tried to remember when last she'd had her period. Brodie counted back and pursed her lips. She'd be okay, she decided. There was no need to panic.

"And?"

Brodie turned to look at Kade standing in the square doorway, still naked, still hot. "It'll be fine. No need to stress, I'm on the pill."

Relief, hot and sure, flooded Kade's face, his eyes. "Good."

Brodie bit her lip, wondering how to phrase her next question. She didn't want to offend him, but…

"Do I need to get myself tested for anything, well, yucky?"

Kade shook his head. "I had a medical three weeks ago and I always use a condom. This is the first time one has broken, I promise."

Well, that was a relief and a less awkward conversation than she'd thought it would be. When Kade grabbed her shirt and pulled her toward him all thoughts of pregnancy and STDs evaporated. He kissed her, long and slow. "You have too many clothes on."

Man, how was she supposed to resist when he made her feel all squirmy and hot? "You don't have any condoms left."

"You do. I saw some in your bathroom cabinet."

Brodie pulled a face. She'd bought them years ago, during her sleeping-with-the-IT-guy phase. "They've been in there for years."

"I checked the expiration date, we're good to go." Kade's lips nibbled her jaw. "You good to go?"

"Bed this time?" Brodie asked.

"And in the shower the next."

Brodie glanced at the clock on her kitchen wall. Twice more in an hour and fifteen minutes?

Well, she'd heard about Kade Webb's ambition, but she'd never thought she'd see it in action.

Kade walked out of her bathroom dressed in his tuxedo pants, his white dress shirt hanging loose. While he was showering she'd run a brush through her hair, pulled on a loose cotton sweater and a pair of yoga pants and was now sitting cross-legged on her bed, trying to act like it was an everyday occurrence for Kade to be in her apartment, showering in her bathroom.

"Why aren't you going to the ball? Surely it's a good place to promote your business?" Kade asked as he sat down next to her to pull on his black socks. "After all, you came to the lunch."

"I came as a sponsor, not to tout for business." Brodie placed her elbows on her knees and her face in her hands. "I've got to be careful how I network. It's not like I can work the room, handing out business cards. My business is based on discretion and most of my clients come to me via word of mouth. Our website and contact numbers are on the program—if someone wants to talk to us they'll call. I only match guys and I can practically guarantee no man there will talk business to me at the ball, not when they can be overheard."

"Would I know any of your clients?"

"More than a couple." Brodie held up her hand. "And no, I'll never tell so don't bother asking."

Kade sent her a quick, assessing look. "I bet a lot of the guys hit on you."

Brodie cocked her head at him. "Why would you think that?"

"So they do, I can see it in your eyes. As for how I know...?" He shrugged. "Say I'm a guy and I'm looking for someone. Then I meet you and think, hey, she's gorgeous and nice, I don't need to look any further. Men are lazy."

"It happens," Brodie admitted.

"How do you deal with them?" Kade pulled on his dress shoes—hand-tooled black leather, Brodie noticed as she scooted off the bed and walked over to her dressing table. She picked up her diamond-and-emerald ring and threw it in his direction.

"Nice ring," he commented and threw it back at her. "Except it's fake."

"As fake as the fiancés I invent every week so I have a good excuse not to date," Brodie replied.

"Ah." Kade bent over to tie his laces and turned his head to look at her. "You've never been tempted?"

Brodie took a moment to consider his question. She was surprised when Kade's eyes narrowed. With jealousy? Not possible.

"My clients are successful, frequently really nice, quite rich men. They drive expensive cars, have gorgeous homes and are intelligent. All very eligible."

Kade scowled.

"But they are also men who are looking to settle down and I am not." Brodie placed her ring back in the shallow bowl holding the jewelry she most often wore. "Besides, becoming involved with a client, in any way, is very unprofessional."

"Good thing I'm not your client, nor will I ever be." Kade sat up and reached for the two sides of his shirt. "I'd rather shoot myself than allow a matchmaker, you or anyone else, to set me up."

Brodie silently admitted she'd rather walk on molten lava than have him as a client.

Kade cocked his head. "So why don't you date?"

Brodie flushed. "Because there are two types of dating. People either date for sex or date for a relationship. I don't do relationships, as a rule. And I very rarely do—" she waved her hand at her bed "—this. I'm as virulently anticommitment as you think you are."

"As I *think* I am?"

Brodie shrugged. She'd seen him with his friends, seen how much he enjoyed his connection with them. He'd be a great husband, a stunning father—if he ever moved out of his party-hearty lifestyle.

Kade held her eyes for a long moment before making a production of looking at his watch. He sent her a crooked grin. "I'm only in it for the hot sex, thanks."

Brodie smiled back. "Then don't win the bid on my auction."

Kade reached into his bag for his bow tie and draped it around his neck, quickly tying it without the use of a mirror. "I very definitely won't," he promised her. "I've got to move or else Wren will have my head."

"Have fun."

Kade picked up his bag and jacket and walked over to her. He dropped a kiss on her temple, then her mouth. "I'd much rather be having fun with you."

Brodie made herself smile. She was pretty sure he said that to all the girls. "'Bye. See you."

"See you," Kade said, walking out of her bedroom. Within seconds she heard her front door open and close and two minutes later, heard the roar of his sports car.

So that was that. She'd had the fantastic sex she'd been craving. But she'd forgotten how much she enjoyed talking to Kade, how easily they slid into intimate conversation. It was as if there were no barriers and it felt way more intimate than post-sex conversation should be. So why on earth was she craving more?

Four

Kade reached for his glass and took a long sip of whiskey. How much longer could this damn ball last?

It was eleven now. If Quinn would move the auction along, Kade could be out of here by midnight. Was it too late to phone Brodie? Was she exhausted? Would he come across as desperate if he called her again so soon? If she was in bed, what was she wearing? A slinky negligee or a tank top and boxer shorts or just her golden skin?

He loved her skin. He loved everything about her body and when he'd held her earlier he'd felt… How had he felt?

Kade cursed the action in his pants. He needed more than a whiskey on ice, he needed a plunge into an ice-fishing hole. At this rate, when he got Brodie where he wanted her—under him—he'd last about two seconds. His reaction to her was ridiculous, insane… There had to be some sort of scientific explanation for why they wanted to rip each other's clothes off at the drop of a hat. Shouldn't the amazing sex they'd shared earlier have taken the edge off? Was it pheromones? Biological instinct? But why her and not one of the many, many good-looking women—many of them Mavericks groupies—scattered throughout the ballroom? None of this made sense.

All he was certain of was that he wanted Brodie again. Urgently. Immediately. Tonight.

Move the hell on, Rayne!

"And now, one of our more interesting donations," Quinn announced. Kade turned his attention back to the stage. "Ms. Brodie Stewart, one of the city's best matchmakers, is offering the opportunity to bid on her matchmaking services. So if you are a guy and are looking for a good woman, Brodie can find one for you." Quinn looked at the Mavericks who occupied the back tables and nodded. "I know one or two, or ten, of my men who should bid."

"I'll bid on a date with Ms. Stewart!" someone shouted from the back. Kade looked down at the photograph of Brodie on the program and couldn't blame the guy for trying his luck. She was gorgeous…

But, for the immediate future, she was *his*.

"She's too smart to date you, Higgins," Quinn warned. "A reminder, this is a matchmaking service for men looking for their perfect woman. So, who is going to give me a hundred dollars?"

Immediately a couple of hands shot up and Kade watched, astounded, as the bids flew up to a thousand dollars, then two. Bids were still bouncing around the room when a cool female voice cut across the hubbub. "Three thousand dollars."

Quinn spun around and his genial smile turned to a scowl. Rory had her paddle raised and was holding his intense stare.

"On whose behalf are you bidding, Rory?" Quinn asked, his frown clearly stating her bidding had better not have anything to do with him.

Kade leaned back in his chair and grinned. Oh, this was going to be fun. Rory had been nagging Quinn about his ability to jump from woman to woman and hobby to hobby—skydiving, white-water rafting, and his obsession with superfast motorcycles—and was determined to nag him into settling down with a wife and two-point-four kids.

She didn't have a hope in hell of changing Quinn. He was even more entrenched in his bachelor lifestyle than Kade. But Kade would enjoy watching her try. He was also damn grateful she was nagging Quinn and not him…

He liked Rory, loved her even, but he wouldn't tolerate her interfering in his life.

Rory's smile was stolen straight from an imp. "Are you taking my bid or not, Rayne?"

Quinn held up two fingers, turned them to his eyes and flipped them around in her direction. "I'm watching you. McCaskill, make sure your woman behaves."

"Yeah, right." Mac leaned back and folded his arms against his chest. "This has nothing to do with me."

"Three-five." A voice from the back got the auction back on track.

"Three-seven," Rory countered.

"Three-eight," Wren calmly stated. She was bidding on behalf of the silent bidders, those who didn't want the room to know they wanted to use a matchmaker.

"Four." Rory waved her paddle in the air.

Four grand? Wow, not bad. The audience obviously loved the notion of being professionally set up.

The bids climbed and Rory matched every one. As the bids went higher, Quinn's face darkened. Oh, yeah, he knew exactly what she was up to. She was buying Brodie's services to find Quinn a woman who would stick around for more than a nanosecond. She was playing with fire, Kade thought, but he couldn't help admiring her moxie.

"Rory," Quinn warned after her bid topped five thousand dollars.

"Quinn," Rory drawled and added another hundred dollars onto her bid.

"You can't bid against yourself," Quinn snapped.

"I just did." Rory's face was alight with laughter. "Oh, I am so going to enjoy this, Rayne. And so will you. So, be a darling. Bang your gavel and tell me I've won."

Quinn looked at Mac. "Doesn't she drive you crazy?"

Mac dropped a kiss on Rory's temple and smiled. "All the time."

Quinn smacked the gavel and told her she'd won the bid before pointing the gavel in her direction. "I won't use it. You can't blackmail me into doing this, Rory."

Rory placed her hand on her heart and batted her eyelashes in his direction. "Quinn, you wound me. I would never dare to set you up." Kade, along with the rest of the guests, leaned forward in their chairs, eager to hear more. "You keep telling me you're not ready for a relationship and I respect that. I do. Besides, wait your turn."

Huh? If this wasn't for Quinn who was she setting up?

"It won't be my turn. *Ever.*" Quinn looked relieved and perplexed at the same time. "So then, pray tell, who is the sacrificial lamb to be led to slaughter?"

Kade smiled at his description as Rory stood up and walked around the table to his side. Oh, crap, oh double crap, he thought as she placed a hand on his shoulder. Kade felt his teeth slam together.

She wouldn't dare. She wasn't that brave.

"Why, who else but one of my favorite people in the whole world? I bought this for my very good friend, Kade Webb." Rory sent Kade a huge smile. As if she could charm him into changing his mind about tossing her from the nearest balcony.

"I just know Brodie will find Kade a stunning woman. I'm counting on her to find someone who'll make him supremely happy."

Dammit, hell, crap.

The room erupted into hoots of laughter and excited chatter. Dammit, hell, crap multiplied.

Kade met Mac's eyes and scowled when his friend raised his glass in a mocking toast. "Welcome to my crazy world, dude."

Kade really liked his best friend's fiancée and thought it wonderful they were having a baby, but his anger over her stunt hadn't disappeared.

What the hell was she thinking? Had she been thinking at all? He didn't need anyone to find him a woman! And he certainly didn't need his current lover to find him a new love!

If he could get past Mac, he had very strong words for Rory. He didn't allow anyone to play fast and loose with his life and he allowed no interference when it came to his sex life. Rory hadn't just stepped over the line, she'd eradicated it.

From his seat in his low-slung German sports car Kade stared at the still dark windows of Brodie's apartment and ran a hand over his jaw. It had taken all his acting skills to breeze through the rest of the evening, to bat away the wisecracks, to laugh at the admittedly good-hearted banter. Well, everyone's banter except his partners' had been good-natured. Mac and Quinn had teased him mercilessly.

For that they would pay...

Kade was perfectly capable of finding his own woman and he didn't want to be in a relationship. Damned women and their meddling. He refused to have anything to do with Rory's scheme and he refused to feel guilty about her wasting her money. She shouldn't have pulled such an asinine trick in the first place!

And if he found out Mac had anything to do with this, then he and McCaskill would go a couple of rounds in the ring, no holds barred.

Kade massaged his temples. It was past 6:00 a.m. He'd had no sleep. He hadn't changed out of his tux. His head was pounding and he wanted nothing more than to climb into bed with Brodie and lose himself in her. He'd done that last night, he remembered. With Brodie the world had disappeared, and for the few hours they were together, he'd relaxed and forgotten. Forgotten about his responsibilities, his past. He'd stopped worrying about his future. With her he'd lived in the moment, something he usually couldn't do.

He wouldn't start to rely on her to feel like that, wouldn't enjoy what they had more than he should. He'd keep it light, he promised himself. This was a one-time, short-term thing. He wasn't looking for long term and neither was she.

All well and good, he thought, but how was he going to handle this stupid situation Rory had placed him in? He had to tell Brodie. That was why he was sitting in front of her apartment complex at the butt crack of dawn.

Brodie had said this—whatever it was between them—would probably be just be one night. And she'd also said something about sleeping with clients being unprofessional.

But if he didn't take up Rory's offer and didn't allow Brodie to set him up, then he wouldn't be her client. He knew their chemistry was combustible enough for more than one night. So everything would be fine. Either way, he had to tell her.

Rory Kydd, if you weren't a woman and if my best friend didn't love you so much, I would kick your very nice ass all over Vancouver.

Maybe he was overthinking this. Brodie was sensible. Kade felt a bit of his panic recede. There was no way she'd accept the challenge to match him. She'd just laugh off Rory's bid and the money would go to charity…no harm, no foul.

He'd call Brodie later, he thought, when he was rested and clearheaded. He lifted his hand to touch the ignition button. His finger hovered there but instead of allowing the powerful engine to roar to life, he instructed his onboard computer to call Brodie.

What are you doing, idiot?

Yet he allowed the cell to ring and eventually he heard Brodie's sleep roughened, sexy voice. "'Lo."

"I'm outside. Let me come up."

"Kade? What time is it?"

"Early." Kade opened the door and climbed out of his expensive car.

He started walking to the front door and his heart jumped when a light snapped on in a corner room on the top floor. She was awake.

Kade flew up the stairs. As he reached her apartment the door opened and Brodie stood in the dark hall, her hair mussed, wearing nothing more than a hockey jersey. His number. Lust and warmth and relief pumped through him. Rory and her machinations were instantly forgotten; his world was comprised of this woman and how desperately he wanted her.

"What's wron—"

Kade cut off Brodie's words by covering her mouth with his. Without ending the kiss, he picked her up, kicked the door shut with his foot and carried her to her bedroom.

They were being perfectly adult about this, Brodie decided as she poured coffee into two mugs. Civilized. So far they'd managed to avoid the awkwardness that normally accompanied the morning after the night before.

He hadn't faked any emotion he didn't feel and she hadn't felt like she was being used. They'd made love, slept a little, made love again and then Kade asked if he could use her shower. She offered to make him breakfast. He declined but said he'd take a cup of coffee.

As extended one-night stands went, it was practically perfect. Then why did she feel like she didn't want it to end?

She was just being silly; she was tired and not thinking straight. After she'd had a solid eight hours of sleep, she'd be grateful Kade was so good at this. Brodie frowned. He'd obviously had a lot of practice.

"Are you going to drink it or just stare at it?"

Brodie turned slowly and sucked in her breath. Kade naked was a revelation, but Kade in a wrinkled tuxedo wasn't too shabby, either. Too shabby as in freakin' damn hot. "Uh…"

Kade walked over to her, lifted the cup to her mouth and tipped it. "Coffee, a magical substance that turns 'uh' into 'good morning, honey.'"

Brodie rolled her eyes as he took her cup and sipped from it. "I'd forgotten you were a morning person. It's okay to kill happy, cheerful morning people, I checked."

Kade handed her cup back and walked over to the pot and poured his own. He leaned his butt against her counter and sipped. "You need a shower and six hours of sleep."

"Eight." Brodie pulled out a wooden chair from the table and dropped into it. "And you're the one who woke me up so early so it's your fault."

Kade grinned. “I didn’t see you fighting me off. Sorry about your panties, by the way.”

“You owe me a new pair,” Brodie told him, both hands wrapped around her cup. Such a nice tuxedo… and it fitted him beautifully. The bow tie was gone and his face was shaded with blond stubble. Then she sat up straighter, remembering why Kade was wearing a tuxedo. “The ball! I’d forgotten… How did it go? Did you manage to raise any money from my donation?”

“Uh, yeah. It sold.”

“You don’t sound too enthusiastic.” Brodie cocked her head. “Didn’t it make any money at all? I’m *so* sorry.”

“It made quite a bit of money. That’s not the problem.”

“There’s a problem? How can there be a problem with my gift? The guy comes to me, I set him up on three dates and hopefully there’s a happily-ever-after.”

“It all depends on who the guy is.”

Right, now she was confused. “So who is the guy?”

“Me.”

She knew it was early and she wasn’t a 100 percent awake, but she thought, maybe, Kade had said *he* was the one she would be working with.

“Please tell me you are joking?” Brodie begged. She knew instinctively that Kade hadn’t had anything to do with her donation. So whose stupid idea was this? "Mac? Quinn?"

"Rory."

So Brodie hadn't misinterpreted Rory's mischievous look after all. Rory was very brave, or very stupid, and obviously very determined to get Kade hitched. Pity she hadn't a clue that Brodie and Kade could spark a wildfire from one kiss.

Damn. She'd just had earth-scorching sex with her client. She'd unwittingly and unknowingly broken her number-one rule. Brodie took a sip of coffee and pushed past the surge of jealousy to work out how, exactly, she was going to do this. Unfortunately there wasn't a manual dealing with the pesky problem of how to match your one-night stand.

God, this was far too confusing for someone whose blood didn't start to circulate until she'd had three cups of coffee. Think this through… Sex, ball for him and sleep for her, sex, client.

Brodie lifted her head to glare at him. Kade had come over to her house and seduced her again, knowing her views about dating her clients. Brodie stood up, anger obliterating the last of her sleepiness.

"How dare you! Why didn't you tell me right away that Rory had bid on my services for you! What the hell, Kade? Did you not think that might have had an impact on my decision to sleep with you again?"

"Whoa, hold on…" Kade lifted his hands.

"You should've told me! I had a right to know, you manipulative jerk!"

"That's not fair."

Brodie brushed past him and tossed her coffee into the sink. "The hell it's not. You knew about this and you knew I'd back off from sleeping with you if you told me. So you didn't say a damn word!"

"I thought about telling you." Kade jammed his hands into the pockets of his pants and scowled.

"*Thought* about it?"

"Yeah! I was going to explain what she'd done, tell you I wasn't going to do it. I was hoping we'd have a laugh about it."

"I'm not finding anything vaguely funny in this."

Kade shoved his hands into his hair, linked his fingers behind his head and stared at her with hot eyes. "I didn't mean to make you feel used, or bad. The truth is that when you opened the door the only thing I could think about was the fact you were nearly naked. I had to have you. Again. Being set up was the last thing on my mind."

She wanted to tell him she didn't believe him, but she saw the truth in his eyes. He'd wanted her like she'd wanted him. Impulsively. Wildly. Crazily. Their need for each other didn't stop to, well, *think*. And, damn, it was hot.

And deeply, utterly problematic. She couldn't control her attraction to him and it seemed Kade was having a similar problem. Such need wasn't healthy, nor was it easy to resist. She needed to step back, to create some distance between them, but every time they were in the same room all they wanted to do was rip off each other's clothes.

They had to stop the madness—this was supposed to be a one-night fling. They were already on day two—sort of—and Kade was like any other man: he wasn't going to walk away from fabulous sex.

She didn't want to walk away from it, either, but for her, being with him felt like it was about more than just the sex. With him she felt alive and vibrant and animated and she couldn't afford to feel like that, even if it only happened in the bedroom. She might come to like it and, worse, get used to it. How would she get that genie back in its bottle?

So this had to stop now. She liked her life exactly as it was. Bland, safe, predictable.

She needed to walk away, far, far away. But Kade just needed to kiss her and she'd be all *yes, please, take me now.*

So she was going to match him.

"You're making too big a deal of this, Brodie," Kade stated. "Just tell Rory we are seeing each other, that there's a conflict of interest. Tell her to let you match Quinn."

Ha! Right. Kade would get out of the matchmaking, keep sleeping with Brodie and annoy Quinn in the process. For Kade, it would be a trifecta win.

But that wasn't going to happen. Brodie shoved aside the heat and the lust and ordered herself to use her brain.

"That would be rude and disrespectful. No, Rory's bid was for you so I will match you."

If she hadn't been feeling so miserable she would've laughed at his horrified face. "What? No!"

Her thinking hat firmly in place, Brodie paced the free area in her small kitchen. "Wren is a smart cookie and I bet she's already thinking of ways to spin this to generate PR for you. Mavericks fans will lap it up. They need a feel-good story, what with the owner's recent death and the future of the team still up in the air. And you released one of their favorite players last month. They are not happy with *you*."

"You seem to know a lot about my business."

Brodie waved away his comment, not feeling the need to tell him that after he left last night she jumped online to read about him and the Mavericks.

"I had solid reasons for releasing him," Kade argued. "It didn't matter that he was the best rookie in the league, a BC native and one of the first graduates from the Mavericks Ice Hockey Academy. He was photographed snorting coke, he was underperforming as a player and he was undisciplined. He had more chances than most, not that the fans care about that." Kade's tone was flat, his eyes bleak.

It had been a joint decision to boot the player, but as CEO, Kade took the flak. He led from the front, Brodie realized, and she had to admire him for that.

Quickly, she returned to the topic at hand. She couldn't afford to get sidetracked *admiring* him.

"Matching you would be good publicity, for the Mavericks and for me."

"Not happening."

"Go to the office, see what Wren's working on. I guarantee it's something similar to what I've been thinking."

A muscle jumped in Kade's jaw and he tipped his head back to look at the ceiling. "I'm going to kill Rory, I really am. Want to help me bury her body?"

At his rueful words the rest of Brodie's anger dissipated. "I'll dig the grave."

Brodie raked her hair back from her face, then grabbed her mug from the sink and poured coffee back into the cup. She took a couple of sips. "I'm sure this is the most interesting conversation after a one-night stand in the history of one-night stands."

Kade rolled his head and Brodie assumed he was trying to work out the tension in his neck. "It's not exactly the conversation I planned on having."

Brodie's heart bounced off her ribs. She shouldn't voice the words on her lips but she had to—it would drive her nuts if she didn't. "What would you have said?"

Kade stepped closer and curled his hand around her neck. "I would've said that I had a great time and I would've asked if we could do this again."

Yeah, that's what she'd thought and that's exactly what she couldn't do. She'd liked it too much, liked having him around. She needed distance and a lot of it. Matching him would give her that.

"We can't," Brodie whispered. "It's too complicated. And, if I'm going to be setting you up…too weird."

"That's not confirmed yet. I'll try my damnedest to get out of it."

He'd come around, Brodie realized. It was too good a story to pass up, too good an opportunity to give the fans something to smile about. And Kade always, always put the Mavericks first.

Kade pulled her forward so her cheek lay against his chest. "If I do this, and I'm not saying I will, when it's done, can we…?"

Brodie knew she should just kill this…thing between them but she simply couldn't. "Let's just play it by ear." She pulled back and looked up at him, forcing her lips to curve into a smile. "You never know, one of those women might be the love of your life and another one-night stand with me will be the last thing on your mind."

"Not freakin' likely," Kade retorted.

Brodie stepped away and folded her arms, trying to remove herself from him mentally and physically. She had to stop *feeling* and keep *thinking.* "We will have to meet professionally, though. I need information from you to find out what you are looking for."

Kade glared at her. "You're talking like this is a done deal! If this happens, be very clear, I'm not looking for *anything*, with anybody! Find me three women who are marginally intelligent, someone who I can talk to for two hours over dinner."

"This is my business, Kade. If we do this, we will do it properly..."

Kade swore and started to roll back his sleeves, revealing the muscles and raised veins in his forearms. Brodie imagined those hands on another woman's skin and felt sick. Now she was adding jealousy to her messy heap of tangled emotions? Wasn't there enough crazy on that pile?

She took a breath. Seeing him with someone else would be good for her. It would put even more distance between them. And that was what she was trying to do here.

"That's the way I work, Kade. It's not up for negotiation."

"Dammit, crap, hell," Kade muttered another string of swearwords under his breath as he finished rolling up his other sleeve. When he was done, he placed his hands on either side of Brodie's face, gave her a hard kiss and picked up his jacket. "We'll talk about this again."

Brodie touched her lips as he walked out of her kitchen, leaving as quickly as he'd arrived.

So that was that. Well, then.

She was now Kade's matchmaker.

Five

Three weeks later Brodie sat in her usual seat at Jan's waiting for Kade, her trusty tablet on the table in front of her. How was she supposed to ask Kade all these intensely personal questions knowing he'd touched, caressed and kissed every inch of her body?

What had she done to piss off the karma fairy?

Brodie placed her cheek in her hand and swallowed down her nausea. Her stomach roiled and she tasted bile in the back of her throat every time she thought about this upcoming interview. She'd had twenty-one days, thanks to Kade's insane schedule and Wren wanting maximum publicity, to feel this way. Three weeks of restless sleep, of feeling on edge, miserable.

Angry.

Once you've done this interview and you've entered the relevant data into the program, you can find his three dates and get on with your life.

Her donation to the auction only included three matches. She wouldn't have to set him up again if none of those woman suited. One batch, she decided, was enough.

And then, when it was done, she'd walk away for good and Kade Webb would be a memory of the best sex she'd ever experienced.

As she'd predicted, Wren had made a charming PR story of Rory's matchmaking gift. Every few weeks, depending on Kade's schedule, a new "date" for Kade would be introduced to the public. Their likes and dislikes would be posted on the Mavericks' website with their photos. Pictures and short video clips of their date would be uploaded and the public could comment. Once all three women had been on a date with Kade, the public would vote on their favorite match.

Such fun and games, Brodie thought. Brodie slipped out of her lightweight cardigan and draped it over her bag. It was hot in the coffee shop, something she'd never experienced before. Usually the air-conditioning made her feel chilly. She also had a headache; damn, she hoped she wasn't getting sick again. That was all she needed.

Brodie heard the tinkle of the chimes announcing a new arrival into the coffee shop. She looked toward the door and immediately sighed. Kade embodied business casual in his dark gold chinos, steel-gray jacket and checked shirt under a sweater the color of berries. Successful and urbane. Too sexy for words.

And she wasn't the only one reacting to his arrival. She felt the collective intake of female breath and knew many sets of ovaries were shivering in delight. Kade pushed his sunglasses onto the top of his head and looked around. He smiled when he saw her and her heart stumbled. Stupid organ.

Kade bent down and brushed his lips across her cheek, and she inhaled his cologne. Sandalwood and spice and something all Kade. She felt her nipples prickle and cursed. Yep, the attraction hadn't lessened one damn bit.

Annoyed she couldn't control her reaction to this man, she frowned at him. "You're late."

"Two minutes and hello to you, too," Kade replied as he sat down. He leaned forward and gripped her chin. "Why are you looking tired? And pale?"

So nice to know she was looking her best, Brodie thought. "I'm fine."

"You sure?"

"I had a chest infection shortly before the auction, maybe it's coming back."

"Are you coughing? Short of breath? Should you see a doctor?"

"I'm fine, Webb. Jeez, stop fussing." She pulled her tablet toward her, hitting the power button. "Shall we get started?"

"Tired and pale and *grumpy.* Can I order some coffee first?" Kade tapped her hand with his finger and waited until she met his eyes. "This situation is crazy enough without us snapping at each other."

She heard the rebuke in his voice and blushed. She was acting like a child. Okay, it wasn't the ideal situation, but she shouldn't be taking her bad mood out on him. He didn't want to be set up any more than she wanted to set him up and he was right, it would be a lot easier if she acted like an adult, even better if she could be friendly.

Pull yourself together, Stewart.

Brodie straightened her shoulders and sent him an apologetic smile. "Sorry. Hi…how are you?"

Kade nodded. "Good. Sorry we haven't been able to meet before this but I've been swamped."

Brodie had realized that. If the papers weren't talking about his upcoming dates, then they were discussing the Mavericks' purchase of Josh Logan, superstar wing, the negotiations to buy the franchise and the legal action against the Mavericks for unfair dismissal by the former star rookie. "What do your lawyers say?"

"About the dismissal?" Kade asked to clarify. He shrugged. "He's wasting his time, and mine, but we all know that. He doesn't have a leg to stand on. It's just a pain in my ass, to be frank." Kade scowled at her tablet. "As are these stupid dates. Seriously, Brodie, I don't want to answer your questions…just choose three women and let's get it over with. Nobody will know but us."

She wished she could but it went against her nature to cut corners. Besides, her questionnaire revealed a lot about her clients and she was curious about Kade.

Not professional, but what the hell? They'd never date and this was the only way she'd be able to assuage her curiosity. "I can't enter the data until I have the answers and I can't match you until I have the data."

"How long does it take?" Kade demanded as Jan approached their table.

"An hour for the long version, half hour if you only answer the compulsory questions." Brodie looked at Jan. "Kade, this is my friend Jan. Jan, Kade Webb."

"I figured." Jan shook his hand. "What can I get you, Kade? Brodie here usually has a coffee milk shake."

Brodie shuddered. She couldn't stomach it today. Too rich…

"Not today, Jan. I'll just have a glass of water."

Jan frowned at her. "You okay?"

"I'm feeling a little flu-ey," Brodie reluctantly admitted. "Hot, a little dizzy and I have a headache." Jan put her hand on her forehead and Brodie slapped it away. "I don't have a temperature and I'll see a doctor if I start coughing, okay?"

"When did you last eat?" Jan demanded.

Maybe that was what was wrong with her. She'd had soup for supper last night and she'd skipped breakfast. She was, she realized, starving. A hamburger would chase away her malaise. "I am hungry." She turned to Kade. "Jan's hamburgers can cure anything from depression to smallpox. Do you want one?"

Kade nodded. "I can eat."

Brodie ordered two cheeseburgers with everything and when Jan left, Brodie smiled at Kade. "Her burgers are really good." She reached into her bag, pulled out her reading glasses and slid them onto her face. "Shall we get started?"

Kade had never considered glasses to be sexy but Brodie's black-rimmed frames turned her green eyes, already mesmerizing, to a deep emerald. He loved her eyes, he thought as he answered questions about his date of birth, his height, his weight. Then again, he also loved her high cheekbones, her stubborn chin, her small but very firm breasts and those long, slim legs.

He liked everything about her and he wished he could blow off lunch and take her to bed. When this stupidity was over, he promised himself. When it was done, he'd kidnap Brodie for the weekend, take her somewhere private and keep her naked in his bed until he'd burned this craving for her out of his system.

He was hardly sleeping and when he did, his

dreams were erotic, with Brodie taking the starring role. He thought about her at the most inappropriate times. Memories from the night they shared obliterated his concentration. It was torture trying to negotiate when he recalled the way Brodie fell apart under his touch.

Brodie pinching his wrist pulled him back to their conversation. "What?"

"I asked…siblings?"

"None." He'd always wanted a brother, someone to take the edge off the loneliness growing up. Someone to stand by his side as he entered the hallway of a new school or joined a new team. Someone who could help him recall the towns they'd lived in and in what order.

"Parents?"

"My father lives in the city, my mother died when I was ten." He snapped the words out. He rubbed a hand over his jaw. God, he didn't want to do this. He never discussed his childhood, his past, his on-off relationship with his socially inept, now reclusive father. "You don't need information about my past so move along."

He saw the furrow appear between Brodie's eyebrows. Well, tough. His childhood was over. He finally had his brothers in Mac and Quinn and he was content. Sometimes he was even happy.

Kade leaned back in his seat. If he had to answer personal questions, then so did she. "And your parents? Where are they?"

"Dead." Brodie didn't lift her head. "I was twenty."

"I'm sorry, Brodes."

"Thanks. Moving on…what characteristic in a woman is most important to you? Looks, empathy, humor, intelligence?"

"All of them," Kade flippantly answered, wishing he could ask how her parents died, but he could tell the subject was firmly off-limits. "Do you have siblings?"

"No." Brodie tapped her fingernail against the screen of her tablet. "I'm asking the questions, Webb, not you."

"Quid pro quo," Kade replied. "Were you close to your parents?"

He saw the answer in her eyes. Sadness, regret, sheer, unrelenting pain. A glimmer suggesting tears was ruthlessly blinked away. Oh, yeah…they might've passed many years ago, but Brodie was still dealing with losing them.

He was fascinated by this softer, emotional Brodie. She was fiercely intelligent, sexy and independent, but beneath her tough shell she made his protective instincts stand up and pay attention. He wanted to dig deeper, uncover more of those hidden depths.

"Tell me about them, Brodie."

"Where is our food?" Brodie demanded, looking around. "I could eat a horse."

"Why won't you talk about them?" Kade persisted. And why couldn't he move off the topic? He never pushed this hard, was normally not this interested. Maybe he was getting sick? He was definitely sick of this matchmaking crap and he hadn't even started with the dates yet. He just wanted to take Brodie home and make love to her again. Was that too much to ask?

Apparently it was.

Brodie finally, finally looked at him and when she did, her face was pale and bleak. "Because it hurts too damn much! Satisfied?"

Dammit, he hadn't meant to hurt her. Brodie flung herself backward and stared out the window to watch the busy traffic.

"Sorry, sweetheart," he murmured.

"Me, too." Brodie, reluctantly, met his eyes. "Please don't pry, Kade. I don't talk about my past."

Maybe she should. Someone, he realized, needed to hear her story and she definitely needed to tell it. It was a shock to realize he wanted to be the one to hear her tale. He wanted to be her friend, to offer comfort. To find out what made her tick.

Jan approached them with two loaded plates. She set the first one down on the table in front of Brodie and then put a plate in front of him. If the burger tasted as good as it smelled, then he was in for a treat, he thought, as he snagged a crispy fry and shoved it into his mouth.

He reached for the salt and frowned when he saw Brodie's now white face. She stared at her plate and, using one finger, pushed it away.

"What's wrong?" he demanded. "I thought you said you were hungry?"

"I was, not anymore." Brodie swallowed and reached for her water. "I think I am definitely getting sick. I'm hot and feeling light-headed."

Jan narrowed her eyes at her, then silently, and without argument, picked up Brodie's plate. Kade didn't understand the long, knowing look Jan sent Brodie and he didn't give her another thought after she walked away.

He frowned when Brodie picked up her tablet and swiped her finger across the screen. "Just choose three women, Brodie, I'm begging you. Any three."

Brodie, who, he was discovering, could give lessons in stubbornness to mules, just shook her head. "Not happening. So here we go..."

Do you base your life decisions more on feelings or rational thinking?

Are you more extroverted or introverted?

Is your bedroom, right now, messy or neat?

Are you more driven or laid-back in your approach to life?

After twenty-five minutes, Kade had a headache to match hers.

A week later Brodie tucked her wallet back into her tote bag and stuffed her phone into the back pocket of her oldest, most comfortable Levi's. Slinging her tote over her shoulder, she took a long sip of the bottled water she'd just purchased and ignored the craziness of the airport. Brodie looked up at the arrivals board, thankful Poppy's flight had landed fifteen minutes ago. Brodie really didn't want to spend her Saturday morning hanging around waiting.

As per usual, there were no empty seats.

Brodie shook her head and headed for a small piece of wall next to a bank of phone booths. Propping her tote behind her back, she placed her booted foot up on the wall, leaned her head back and closed her eyes. God, she couldn't remember when last she'd felt this overwhelming tiredness.

She was overworked, run-down, stressed out. Maybe she was flirting with burnout. She'd been working fourteen- and sixteen-hour days for the last few weeks, partly to keep up with her ever increasing client list. The publicity around Kade had resulted in a surge of business. Work was also an excellent way to stop thinking—obsessing—about Kade.

She really didn't like the amount of space he was renting in her brain. And she wished she could just make a decision on who was going to be his first date. She knew she was being ultra picky but she couldn't help it. She wanted pretty but not blow-your-socks-off attractive. She wanted a good conversationalist but not someone who was intriguing. She wanted smart but not too smart.

She didn't want him to date anyone at all.

Which was ludicrous—she had no claim on the man and hadn't she decided they needed some distance? God, maybe she was the source of her own exhaustion. Donating to the charity auction had not been one of her smarter ideas. Sure, it was a good cause, but following up her one-night stand with finding her said ONS someone else to have a one-night stand with left a sour taste in her mouth.

Brodie silently urged her great-aunt to hurry up. Poppy had the energy and enthusiasm of a ten-year-old with a tendency to talk to everyone she encountered. Brodie wondered how long Poppy would be staying in town before the travel bug bit again. She'd visited more countries in three years than most people did in a lifetime and Brodie couldn't help but admire her great-aunt's sense of adventure. It took courage to travel on her own and to make friends along the way.

Just hurry yourself up, Poppy. I really am feeling, well, like hell. And the sooner we get out of here, the happier I'll be.

A cramping stomach accompanied Brodie's nausea. She clenched her jaw and clutched her stomach, frantically thinking about what she had recently eaten that could have given her food poisoning. Cornflakes? Last night's boiled egg?

Brodie took a series of deep breaths, sucked on some more water and felt the nausea recede. When she opened her eyes again she saw Poppy, one hand on her travel case and the other on her hip, a speculative look on her face.

Brodie managed a wan smile. "Hey, you're here.

That was quick." She kissed Poppy's cheek and gave her a long hug. "How was Bali?"

"Loved it," Poppy replied. "I was considering staying another month but then I was invited to join a cruise to Alaska leaving in the next month."

"You're leaving again?"

Poppy dropped into a recently vacated empty seat. "You look dreadful. Are you sick?"

"Yeah, so nauseous. I must've eaten something bad last night.

Poppy grinned. "Unless you've discovered sex in the last six weeks and someone has dropped a bun in your oven. But that's not likely since you have the world's most boring sex life."

Brodie stared at her great-aunt while Poppy's words sank in.

No, no… God, *no*!

"I'm not pregnant." Brodie ground out the words, pushing back her hair. She wasn't even going to consider such a ridiculous scenario. She was on the pill! Brodie scrabbled in her bag for another bottle of water and after trying to open it with a shaking hand, passed it over to Poppy for help twisting off the cap. Brodie felt her body ice up with every drop she swallowed.

"Pregnancy would explain how you are feeling and is a result of sex. So, have you had any lately?"

Admitting to sex made the possibility of her being pregnant terribly real. "One time, weeks ago. The condom split."

"Ah, that would explain it."

"It explains nothing! I'm on the pill!"

"Even the pill can fail sometimes."

Brodie lowered the bottle and started to shake. Could she possibly be pregnant with Kade's baby?

From a universe far away Brodie felt Poppy's hand on her back. "Come on, Mata Hari, let's find you a pregnancy test and you can tell me who, what, where and when."

Three pregnancy tests could not be wrong. Unfortunately.

It had taken a week of Poppy's nagging for Brodie to find her courage to do a pregnancy test and now she desperately wished she hadn't.

Brodie stared at the three sticks lined up on the edge of her bathroom counter and hoped her Jedi mind trick would turn the positive signs to negative. After five minutes her brain felt like it was about to explode so she sat down on the toilet seat and placed her head in her hands.

She was pregnant. Tears ran down her face as she admitted that Poppy had called it—the girl who had the sex life of a nun was pregnant because Kade Webb carried around a faulty condom.

Jerk. Dipstick. Moron.

Brodie bit her lip. What was the moron/jerk/dipstick doing tonight? It was Saturday. He might be on a date with one of her suggestions for his first date. Which one? The redhead with the engineering degree? The blonde teacher? The Brazilian doctor? Brodie pulled her hair. If she thought about Kade dating, she'd go crazy.

Maybe, instead of feeling jealous of those women, it would be sensible to consider the much bigger problem growing inside her. The exploding bundle of cells that would, in a couple of weeks, become a fetus and then a little human, a perfect mixture of Kade and her.

She wasn't ready to be a mommy. Hell, she wasn't ready—possibly wouldn't ever be ready—for a relationship. And motherhood was the biggest relationship of them all. It never ended. Until death…

Brodie felt the room spin and knew she was close to panicking. She couldn't be responsible for another life. She couldn't even emotionally connect to anyone else. How would she raise a well-balanced, well-adjusted kid with all her trust and loss and abandonment issues?

How could she raise a kid at all? She couldn't do this. She didn't have to do this. It was the twenty-first century and if she wanted, she could un-pregnant herself. Her life could go back to what it was before… She could be back in control. She wouldn't have to confront Kade. She wouldn't have to change her life. By tomorrow, or the day after, she'd be back to normal.

Brodie stood up and looked at her pale face in the mirror. Back to normal. She wanted normal… Didn't she? She wanted smooth, unemotional, uncluttered. She wasn't the type who wanted to sail her ship through stormy seas. She'd experienced the tempests and vagaries and sheer brutality of life and she didn't want to be on another rocking boat.

Right. Sorted. She had a plan. So why wasn't she feeling at peace with the decision? Why did she feel at odds with herself and the universe?

"You can't hide in there forever." Poppy's voice drifted under the door. Brodie reached over and flipped the lock. Within ten seconds Poppy's keen eyes saw the tests and the results. Poppy, being Poppy, just raised her eyebrows. "What are you going to do?"

Brodie lifted her shoulders and let them hover somewhere around her ears. It would help to talk this through with someone and since Poppy was here Brodie figured she was a good candidate. "I'm thinking about—" she couldn't articulate the process,"—becoming un-pregnant."

If she couldn't *say* it, how was she going to *do* it?

Poppy, unmarried by choice, didn't react to that statement. "That's one option," she stated, crossing her arms over her chest, her bright blue eyes shrewd.

"Raising a child by myself is not much of an option," Brodie snapped.

"Depends on your point of view," Poppy replied, her voice easy. "Your parents thought you were the best thing to hit this planet and they had you in far more difficult circumstances than you are in now."

Brodie frowned. "I'll be a single mother, Poppy. My parents were together."

"They were married, yes, but your father was in

the army, stationed overseas. Your mom was alone for six, eight months at a time and she coped. Money was tight for them." Poppy looked at Brodie's designer jeans and pointed to her expensive toiletries. "Money is not an object for you. You are your own boss and you can juggle your time. You could take your child to work or you could start working more from home. This is not the disaster you think it is."

Brodie tried to find an argument to counter Poppy's, but she came up blank. Before she could speak, Poppy continued. "Your parents were practically broke and always apart and yet they never once regretted having you. They were so excited when you came along."

Brodie's mom had loved kids and had wanted a houseful but, because she'd had complications while she was pregnant with Brodie, she'd had to forgo that dream. "I can't wait until you have kids," she'd tell Brodie. "I hope you have lots and I'll help you look after them."

Except you are not here when I need you most. You won't be here to help and I'll have to do it... alone.

Poppy wouldn't give up her traveling to become a nanny. Besides, knowing Poppy, she'd probably leave the baby at the supermarket or something.

"What about the man who impregnated you?"

"You make me sound like a broodmare, Pops," Brodie complained, pushing her hand into her hair. She looked around and noticed they were having this life-changing discussion in her too-small bathroom. "And why are we talking in here?"

"Because I'm standing in the doorway and you can't run away when the topic gets heated."

"I don't run away!" Brodie protested. Though, in her heart, she knew she did.

Poppy rolled her eyes at the blatant lie. "So, about the father."

"What about him?" Brodie demanded.

"Are you going to tell him?"

Brodie groaned. "I don't know what the hell I am going to do, Poppy!"

Poppy crossed one ankle over the other and Brodie saw she'd acquired a new tattoo in Bali, this one on her wrist. "I think you should talk to him. The decision lies with you but he was there. He helped create the situation and he has a right to be part of the solution."

"He doesn't have to know, either way."

"Legally? No. Morally? You sure?" Poppy asked.

Brodie tipped her head up to look at the ceiling. "I was at the point of making a decision," Brodie complained. "Thank you for complicating the situation for me, Great-aunt."

"Someone needs to," Poppy muttered, looking exasperated. She pointed a long finger at Brodie's face. "Your problem is that since your parents and friends died, you always take the easy route, Brodie."

"I do not!"

"Pfft. Of course you do! Not having this baby is

the easy way. Not telling the father is the easy way. Living in this house and burying yourself in your work—finding other people love but not yourself!—is taking the easy route. You need to be braver!"

"I survived a multicar pileup that wiped out my parents and best friends!" Brodie shouted.

"But it didn't kill *you*!" Poppy responded, her voice rising, too. "You are so damn scared to risk being hurt that you don't live! You satisfy your need for love by setting up other people. You keep busy to stop yourself from feeling lonely, and you don't do anything exciting or fun. Do you know how thrilled I am to find out that you've had a one-night stand? I think it's brilliant because someone finally jolted you out of your safety bubble. And, dammit, I hope you are brave enough to talk to the father, to have this kid, because I think it will be the making of you."

Through Brodie's shock and anger she saw Poppy blink back tears. Poppy was the strongest person she knew and not given to showing emotion. "I want you to be brave, Brodie. I want you to start living."

Brodie felt her anger fade. "I don't know how," she whispered. "I've forgotten."

Poppy walked toward her and pulled her to her slight frame. "You start by taking one step at a time, my darling. Go talk to the father..." Poppy pulled back to frown at Brodie. "Who is the father?"

"Kade Webb."

"My baby has taste." Poppy grinned. "Well, at the risk of sounding shallow, at the very least the baby will be one good-looking little human." Poppy grabbed Brodie's hand and pulled her from the bathroom. "Now come and tell me how you met and, crucially, how you ended up in bed."

Six

Date one of three and he was officially off the publicity wagon until he had to do this again next month.

Well, he would be done as soon as she left his apartment. He wouldn't offer her any more wine, Kade decided. He wasn't going to extend the date any longer than he absolutely had to. He'd wanted to have supper at a restaurant but Wren had insisted he cook Rachel dinner in his expansive loft apartment. Cooking her dinner would show the public his caring, domestic side.

The public, thanks to the photographers who'd hovered around, would also see his residence in downtown Vancouver and Simon, his mutt. Kade stroked his hand over Si's head, which lay heavy on his thigh. Simon, whom he'd found in an alley on one of his early-morning runs, considered Kade his personal property and any woman would have to fight his dog for a place in his life.

Kade stifled his sigh and resisted the urge to look at his watch. When he'd received the portfolios of his potential dates from Brodie, he'd flipped through the three candidates and opted to eat with the doctor. Then he'd contacted Wren and instructed her to arrange his first date for as soon as possible. Breakfast, lunch and supper…whenever, she just had to get it done. Wren, efficient as always, had done exactly that. One down, two to go.

"And then I spent three months working in the Sudan with Médecins Sans Frontières."

His buzzer signaled someone was downstairs wanting to come up. Kade smiled at his guest, hoping Wren had read his mind and come to rescue him.

You're a big boy, he heard Wren's amused voice in his head. *If you can talk them into bed, then you sure as hell don't need my help to talk them out of your apartment.*

Or maybe it was Quinn downstairs. The doctor was his type—brainy and built. Quinn would, if Kade asked him, take Rachel off his hands. Kade stood up and walked across the open space to his front door and intercom. He pressed the button, called out a greeting and shrugged when no one answered.

It had to be Mac or Quinn. They both usually hit the buzzer to signal they were on their way up.

Kade turned to walk back to his guest. It was definitely time to maneuver her out the door. Please let Quinn be thundering up the steps, he thought. *Please.*

A tentative knock told him it wasn't Quinn, or Mac, and Kade frowned. Who else would be visiting him at 9:45 p.m. on a Saturday night? Then again, whoever it was would be a distraction and he'd take what he could get.

Sending a fake smile of apology in Rachel's direction, he walked back to the door and opened it. As per usual when he saw Brodie, his mouth dried up and his heart flipped once, then twice.

What was it about this woman that turned his brain to mush? If he compared her to Rachel, Brodie came up short. She was wearing ratty jeans and a tight T-shirt in pale gray, a perfect match to her complexion. Pale gray tinged with green. Her eyes were a flat, dark, mossy green and accessorized by huge black rings. Her hair was raked off her face and she looked like a spring ready to explode.

"We need to talk… Can I come in?"

Kade tossed a look over his shoulder and sighed when he saw Rachel walking in their direction, a puzzled look on her face. "Hi, there." Rachel appeared at his shoulder and he watched Brodie's eyes widen as she gave the buxom doctor a good up-and-down look.

"Doctor Martinez." Brodie's voice cooled.

Brodie stepped to the side and looked across his apartment to the small dining table at the far end of the room. Kade sighed. Fat candles, muted light, wineglasses, her heels next to her chair. It looked like everything it really wasn't, a romantic dinner for two.

Kade heard the click of Si's nails against the wooden floor and waited for the dog to take his customary place at Kade's side. Si, to Kade's surprise, walked straight past him and up to Brodie. Kade waited for the growl and cocked his head when Simon nuzzled his snout into Brodie's hand. Brodie immediately, and instinctively, dropped to her haunches and rubbed her hands over Si's ears and down his neck.

Delight flickered in her tired eyes. "Oh, he's gorgeous, Kade. I didn't know you had a dog."

"We haven't exactly had a lot of time to talk," Kade pointed out and Brodie flushed. "Meet Simon, part Alsatian, part malamute, all sappy. I've had him about two months."

"He's a lovely dog," Rachel said, her tone bright and chirpy. Oh, hell, he'd forgotten she was there.

Kade watched as Brodie stood up slowly, a blush creeping up her neck. Kade could see she was ready to bolt. He wanted to hustle Rachel out, pull Brodie in, pick her up and cradle her in his arms and find out, in between kisses, what was making her so very miserable.

Because she was—he knew it like his own name.

Brodie darted a look at Rachel and he saw her

suck in a breath. He watched how she added two and two and somehow ended up with sixty-five.

Brodie lifted her hands and stepped back. "I am being inexcusably rude, I'm so sorry." She gave them a smile as fake as this date.

"But you said you needed to talk," Kade reminded her. "I'm sure Rachel will excuse us."

"Please… It's really not important," Brodie insisted and jammed her hands into the back pockets of her jeans. "I'm so sorry to have disturbed your evening. Good night."

"Brodie." Kade didn't want her to leave.

"Good night!" Rachel called, turning and walking back to the table. He watched, irritated, as she picked up his full glass of wine to take a healthy sip. She cradled the glass between her ample breasts and sent him a speculative look.

Kade stopped by the coatrack and pulled her bag and jacket from a hook and held them out to her.

Rachel put down her wine and cocked her head. A small, regretful smile tilted her wide mouth upward.

"Well, that sucks," she cheerfully stated, suddenly looking a lot warmer. Kade scratched his forehead in confusion. But before he could ask for an explanation, Rachel spoke again. "Want to tell me why you are doing the dating thing when you are completely besotted with your matchmaker?"

"I am not besotted with her!" Kade responded, thoroughly disconcerted by the observation.

"Well, something is happening between you two."

Rachel slipped into her shoes, then walked over to him and took her jacket and purse from his hands. "Pity, because I rather like you."

Kade rubbed his hand across his forehead. "Look, I enjoyed our evening..."

Rachel laughed. "Oh, you big, fat liar! I've never worked so hard in all my life to impress someone and most men are easily impressed!"

He had to smile and was so damn thankful he wasn't dealing with the drama queen he'd expected her to be. "I'm so sorry. I'm really not besotted with her but it *is* complicated. And these dates are..." Could he trust her not to spill the beans?

"A publicity stunt?" Rachel had guessed before he could say more. "I figured that out as soon as I saw the look on your face when you opened the door. Don't worry, I won't say anything."

Kade let out a relieved sigh. "Thank you." He bent down and placed a kiss on her cheek. "I really appreciate it. I'll take you home."

Rachel patted his biceps. "I'll call a cab and you can go and find your girl so that you can sort out your complications."

Kade watched her walk out of his loft, resisting the urge to deny there was anything between him and Brodie besides some great sex and a couple of laughs. There was nothing to sort out, nothing to worry about. If that was the case, then he shouldn't be desperate to find out exactly what it was Brodie wanted to say.

He was just curious, he told himself. It didn't mean he had feelings for her. He wasn't besotted with her.

Besotted? What a ridiculous word! He wasn't… He couldn't be. He didn't *do* besotted. But he would admit to being curious, that wasn't a crime.

Brodie left the rain forest and the Willowbrae Trail and walked onto one of the vast, sandy beaches characterizing this part of the west coast of Vancouver Island. She stared at the huge waves rolling in from Japan and slipped out of her sneakers, digging her toes into the cool sand.

This place—Poppy's cabin—with its magnificent sea views, was her hideout, the place she ran to every time her life fell apart. She and her family had spent many holidays here, in winter and summer and the seasons in between. This was where she felt closest to them. After the accident, she'd spent six weeks up here, to recuperate. Her body healed quickly but her heart never had.

Despite the memories, she still wanted to run up here when life threw her curveballs. Here, if she didn't think too much, her soul felt occasionally satisfied. This was her special place, her thinking place.

Two days had passed since she'd left Vancouver and she'd spent all that time thinking of Kade, and trying *not* to obsess about what happened between him and Doctor Delicious after Brodie left.

The thought of him and another woman so soon—was six weeks soon?

And she still had to tell him about the pregnancy. Brodie placed her hands on her stomach and sucked in a breath. She also needed to tell him she intended to keep this child, to raise it on her own.

Poppy was right. Keeping the baby would take courage and sacrifice and…well, balls. Brodie also knew her parents would have wanted her to keep the child, to care for the next generation of Stewarts as they'd planned to do.

So she'd decided to be a mommy. She needed to tell Kade he was going to be a daddy. There was no rush, Brodie thought, as she picked up a piece of driftwood and tossed it toward a bubbling wave. She had eight or so months.

Or, hell, maybe not.

Brodie recognized his stride first, long and loose. His blond hair and most of his face was covered by a black cap. Simon, Kade's huge, sloppy mutt, galloped between him and the waves, barking with joy. Then Simon recognized her and let out a yelp of elated welcome. Brodie was glad that he, at least, looked happy to see her.

Kade did not. He stopped in front of her, tipped back the rim of his cap and scowled. "Sixteen missed calls. Six messages, Stewart. Seriously?"

"I needed some time alone," Brodie replied, rubbing Simon's ears. She looked up into Kade's frustrated eyes. "Why are you here?"

The wind blew Kade's cotton shirt up and revealed the ridges of his stomach. Brodie had to stop herself from whimpering. "I'm here because you came to my loft, looking like hell on wheels, saying we needed to talk. I've spent the last two days looking for you."

Brodie picked up a small stick and threw it for Simon, who ran straight past it into a wave. "I suppose Poppy told you where I was."

"When I managed to find her," Kade muttered.

Brodie frowned. "She's not difficult to find. She lives below me."

"Not for the last two nights. She finally came home, on a Harley, with a guy who was at least fifteen years younger than her."

Brodie grinned. "Good for Poppy." At least one of them was having fun.

Brodie felt her throat tighten. She had to tell him, now.

"Kade..." Brodie met his eyes, dug deep and found a little bit of courage. "The night we were together... Do you remember how we brushed off the issue of the split condom?"

Kade frowned and his face darkened. She didn't need to say any more, she could see he'd immediately connected the dots. "You're...?" He rubbed his hands over his face.

"Pregnant," Brodie confirmed.

"But you said you were on the pill," Kade stuttered and the color drained from his face.

"I was on the pill, but apparently it fails sometimes."

Kade linked his hands behind his head. He looked shaken and, understandably, mad as hell. Brodie couldn't blame him; she'd experienced those emotions herself.

"Might I remind you," she added, "the condom *you brought* was faulty."

"So you're saying this is my fault?" Kade shouted, dropping his hands. Simon whined and Kade patted his head to reassure him everything was okay. Brodie wished he'd reassure her, too.

Brodie made an effort to hold on to her own slipping temper. "I'm not blaming you, I'm explaining what happened."

Kade dropped a couple of F-bombs. "I'm not ready to be a father. I don't want to be a father!"

"Being a mother wasn't in my five-year plan, either, Webb."

Kade folded his arms across his chest and glared at her. "You don't seem particularly upset about this."

Where was he the last couple of nights when she'd cried herself to sleep? The same nights she'd paced the floor? "I'm pregnant and it's not something that's going away. I have to deal with it. You, however, do not."

"What the *hell* do you mean?"

Brodie tucked a strand of hair behind her ear and shrugged. "If you want I'll sign a release absolving you of all responsibility for this child."

Kade stared down at the sand and Brodie noticed his hands, in the pockets of his khakis shorts, were now fists. He was hanging on to his temper by a thread. "Is that my only option?"

"What else do you want? You just said you don't want to be this baby's father. Have you changed your mind? That would mean paying child support and sorting out custody arrangements. Is that what you want?"

"For crap's sake, I don't know! I'm still trying to deal with the idea you're saying you're pregnant!" Kade yelled.

"I'm *saying* I am pregnant?" Brodie frowned. Did he think she was making this up for kicks and giggles? "Do you doubt me?" she asked, her voice low and bitter.

"We slept together several weeks ago, how can you be sure?" Kade retorted. "Have you done a blood test? How can I be sure you're not jerking my chain?"

Brodie's mouth fell open. How could he, for one moment, think she would lie about this? Didn't he know her at all? Actually, he didn't, Brodie admitted. They'd shared their bodies but nothing of their thoughts or feelings. And now they were going to have a baby together... No, judging by his lack of enthusiasm, she was going to be walking this road solo.

Brodie slapped her hand on his chest and pushed. He didn't shift a millimeter and her temper bubbled. "I am not lying, exaggerating or jerking your chain! This isn't fun for me, either, Webb, but I'm going to be an adult and deal with it!" Her chest felt tight and her face was on fire. "I've done my part. I've informed you. I'll get my lawyer to draw up a document releasing you from your parental rights."

Brodie spun around and started toward the path leading back to the cabin. God, she was tired. Tired of stressing, tired of arguing. Just plain exhausted. Tired of dealing with the emotions Webb yanked to the surface whenever she was around him. She just wanted some peace, to retreat, to shut down.

"I don't know what I want!" Kade hurled the words and Brodie felt them bounce off the back of her head.

Brodie slowly turned and shrugged. "I can't help you with that. But accusing me of lying certainly doesn't help make sense of the situation."

Embarrassment flashed across Kade's face. He stared at the sand and then out to sea. She could see the tension on his face. "It's happened before...with two other women. They said I made them pregnant."

Brodie tipped her head. "Did you?"

His look was hot and tight and supremely pissed off. "Hell no! When my lawyers asked for DNA proof they backed down."

Of course they did. Brodie sighed and tried to ignore the growing hurt enveloping her heart. "So, naturally, I'm just another one-night stand, another woman you slept with who wants to trap you." She released a small, bitter laugh and lifted her hands in a what-was-I-thinking? gesture. "That's an example of how extraordinarily stupid I can be on occasion. Goodbye, Kade."

Brodie took a couple of steps before turning around once more. "My lawyer will contact yours. I really don't think we have much more to say to one another."

Brodie walked away and Kade didn't call her back, didn't say another word. When she hit the trail to the cottage, Brodie patted her stomach.

So it'll be you and me, babe. We'll be fine.

Of course she would. She always was.

So that wasn't what he'd been expecting, Kade thought as he sank to the sand and stared at the wild waves slapping the beach.

Brodie was pregnant? With *his* child? What the hell…? He scrubbed his face with his hands. What were the chances? And why was fate screwing with him?

Kade stroked Si's head and rubbed his ears. With his busy schedule, just remembering to feed and walk Si was problematic. And life was expecting him to deal with a child?

This was karma, Kade thought. Life coming back to bite him in the ass because he'd been so rude about Mac becoming a father. But Mac had Rory—patient, calm and thinking—to guide him through the process.

Kade didn't have Brodie and, judging by the final sentence she'd flung at him, he didn't need to worry about her or his child. She was prepared to go it alone.

He shouldn't have accused her of lying. Brodie wasn't another bimbo trying to drag a commitment out of him. Brodie didn't want a relationship. She didn't need a man in her life. She was independent and self-sufficient and she was strong enough to raise her child—their child—on her own.

If he wanted to he could walk away, forget about this conversation and forget he had a baby on the way. According to Brodie all he needed to do was sign a piece of paper and his life would go back to normal.

No child.

No Brodie.

Pain bloomed in the area below his sternum and he pushed his fist into the spot to relieve the burn. Could he do it? Could he walk away and not think about her, them, anymore?

Probably.

Definitely.

Not.

He couldn't keep Brodie off his mind as it was. There was something about her that was different from any other woman he'd ever known. He was, on a cellular level, attracted to her, but despite her I-can-handle-whatever-life-throws-at-me attitude, he sensed a vulnerability in her that jerked his protective instincts to life. She also had more secrets than the CIA, secrets he wanted to discover. Oh, he wasn't thinking of her with respect to the long term or a commitment. He hadn't turned *that* mushy and sentimental, but he couldn't dismiss her.

It would be easier if he could.

As for her carrying his child…

He'd always been ambivalent about having children. As a child, his family situation had been dysfunctional at best, screwed up at worst. He'd been an afterthought to his parents and when his mom died, he'd been nothing more than a burden to his head-in-the-clouds father. Practicality had never been his dad's strong suit and, teamed with a wildly impulsive nature, having a ten-year-old was a drag. A kid required food, clothes and schooling, and sometimes his dad hadn't managed any of those. To his father, Kade had been a distraction from his art, a responsibility he'd never signed on for.

Kade felt his jaw lock as the realization smacked him in the face: his child would be a distraction from his own career and a responsibility he'd never signed on for.

Like father, like son.

Except he wasn't his father and he refused to follow in the man's footsteps. It was *his* condom that broke; Kade was as responsible for the pregnancy as Brodie. He took responsibility for his actions, both in his business and in his personal life. He faced life like a man, not like the spoiled child he'd frequently thought his father to be.

And, for some reason, he couldn't get the image of Brodie, soft and round with pregnancy, out of his head. He could see a child sleeping on her chest; he wanted to watch her nursing. Dammit, he could even imagine himself changing a diaper, running after his toddler on a beach, teaching the boy to skate.

For the first time ever, Kade could imagine being part of a family, working for and protecting *his* family. Having his own little tribe.

It wouldn't be like that, really. Of course it wouldn't. Nothing ever worked out like a fairy tale, but it was a nice daydream. He and Brodie weren't going to have the dream but they could have something...different.

He could share the responsibility of raising their child. Taking responsibility meant paying all the bills their child incurred. From pregnancy to college and beyond, he'd supply the cash. Kade hauled in some much-needed air. Cash was the easy part. He had enough to financially support hundreds of kids. The notion of being a *father* had him gasping for air. Being a dad. Because there was a difference; he knew that as well as he knew his own body.

He couldn't be like his father...

Kade never half-assed anything. He didn't cut corners or skimp on the details. He worked. And then he worked some more. He worked at his friendships; he worked at his career. He gave 110 percent, every time.

And he'd give being a dad 110 percent, as well. His child would not grow up feeling like a failure, like an afterthought, like a burden. He wasn't going to perpetuate that stupid cycle.

And if Brodie didn't like that, then she'd better get with the program because that was the way it was going to be. He wasn't going to be a husband or a long-term lover, but he'd be a damn good father and, more importantly, he'd be there every step of the way…

Seven

Brodie placed her heels on the edge of the Adirondack chair and rested her chin on her knees, the expansive view of the Florencia Bay blurry from the tears she refused to let fall. She was used to being alone. She'd made a point of it. But for the first time in nearly a decade she felt like she could do with some help. Just a shoulder to lean on, someone to tell her she could do this, that she was strong enough, brave enough.

She wanted a pair of arms to hold her, someone else's strength to lift her, a little encouragement. This was the downside of being alone, Brodie realized. When you'd consistently kept yourself apart there was no one you could call on. She'd made this bed and now she had to sleep in it.

Alone.

Well, this sucked. Brodie shoved the heels of her hands into her eye sockets and pushed, hoping the pressure would stop the burning in her eyes. That she wanted to cry was utter madness. She was pregnant, not dying. She was financially able to raise this child and give it everything it needed—she had to stop calling it an *it*!—and this situation didn't warrant tears. If memories didn't make her cry, then her pregnancy had no right to. She was stronger than that.

Brodie straightened her shoulders. So she was going to be a single mother, big deal. Millions of women all over the world did it on a daily basis, a lot of them with fewer resources than she had. *Stop being a wuss and get on with it. Rework those plans; write a list. Do something instead of just moping!*

She needed to see a doctor and she needed to contact her lawyer. She needed to stop thinking about stupid Kade Webb and the fact he'd accused her of scamming him.

The jerk! Oh, she so wasn't going to think about him again. From this moment on he was her baby's sperm donor and nothing else.

She simply wasn't going to think about him again.

"Brodie."

Brodie looked up at the clear blue sky and shook her head. "Seriously?"

No one, not God, the universe or that bitch karma, answered her. Brodie reluctantly turned her head and watched Kade walk across the patio toward the other Adirondack chair. Without saying a word, he sat down, rested his forearms on his thighs and dropped his hands between his knees. Simon sat near the edge of the stairs and barked at a seagull flying over his head.

Kade had come straight from the beach, Brodie realized. Sand clung to his feet, which were shoved into expensive flips-flops, and clung to the hair on his bare calves. He had nice feet. Big feet. He was a big guy, *everywhere.*

And it was his *everywhere* that had put her into this situation. She scowled. "What now, Kade?"

Kade turned and looked at her. "I don't want to fight."

"That's fine." Brodie dropped her legs and pointed to the stairs. "So just leave."

"That's not happening, either." Kade calmly leaned back and put one ankle onto his opposite knee. He rolled his shoulders and looked around, taking in the wood, steel and glass cabin and the incredible view. "This place is amazing. Do you own it?"

She had some money but not enough to own a property like this. "Poppy's."

Why was he here? Why was he back? Was he going to take more shots at her? She didn't think she could tolerate any more this morning. She felt nauseous and slightly dizzy and, dammit, she wanted to crawl into his arms and rest awhile.

Huh. So she hadn't wanted just anyone to hold

her, she'd wanted Kade's arms around her. And she'd called *him* a moron? She took the prize.

"What do you want, Kade?" she asked, weary.

"Are you okay?" Kade waved in the direction of her stomach, his brown eyes dark with—dare she think it?—concern. "I mean, apart from the whole being-pregnant issue?"

"Why?"

"You just look, well, awful. You're like a pale green color. You've lost weight and you look like you haven't slept properly in a month."

Nice to know she was looking like a wreck. Especially when the description came from a man who graced the front covers of sports magazines.

"Do you need to see a doctor? Maybe they could run some tests to check if there is something else wrong."

"I'm fine, Webb. I'm pregnant. I puke, a lot. I don't sleep much because I've been stressed out of my head!"

"Stressed about telling me?" Kade asked, linking his hands across his flat stomach.

Brodie stood up and went to the balustrade. "Partly. But that's done so…feel free to leave."

Kade didn't look like he was going anywhere anytime soon. He just held her hot gaze. "I'm sorry I reacted badly." His smile was self-deprecating and very attractive. "Not my best moment."

"Yeah, accusing me of trying to trap you was a

high point," Brodie said, looking toward the beach. "Apology accepted. You can—"

"Go now? Why are you trying to get rid of me?"

"Because I have stuff to do! I need to call my lawyer, see a doctor, plan mine and the baby's future!" Brodie cried.

Kade stood up, walked over to her and touched her cheek with his fingers. "It's not going to be like that, Brodie."

"Like what?" Brodie whispered.

"I know you think you are going to do this alone—because, hell, you like being self-reliant—but I'm in it for the long haul."

"What?" Brodie demanded, thrown off-kilter. What was he talking about?

"I am going to be this baby's father in every way that counts."

Brodie looked at him, aghast. What was happening here? "Wha-at?"

"You're going to have to learn to be part of a team, Brodie, because that's what we are, from this point on." Kade tapped her nose and stood back, his stance casual. But his eyes, dark and serious and oh, so determined, told another story.

"I don't understand."

"I am not going anywhere. We're in this. *Together*."

What? No! She didn't play nicely with others. She had no idea how to work within a team. She was a lone wolf; she didn't function within a pack. And really, what the hell did he think he was doing, acting all reasonable and concerned?

That wasn't going to work for her. She made her own decisions and she didn't like it that with Kade, she wasn't in charge. He might sound laid-back but beneath his charm the man was driven and ambitious and bossy.

But even as she protested his change of heart, she had the warm fuzzies and felt a certain relief she wouldn't be carrying this burden alone.

Even so, she shook her head. "There is no *we*. This baby is my problem, my responsibility."

"This baby is *our* problem, *our* responsibility. Mine as much as yours," Kade replied, not budging an inch. "Quit arguing, honey, because you're not going to win."

Behind her back Brodie gripped the balustrade with both hands. "What does that mean? Are you going to change diapers and do midnight feeds? Are you going to drive around the city trying to get the kid to sleep? Or are you just going to fling some money at me?"

Anger flickered in Kade's eyes. "I'll do whatever I need to do to make your life easier, to be a father. I will support you, and the baby, with money, but more importantly, with my time and my effort. I'm repeating this in an effort to get it to sink into that stubborn head of yours, you are not in this alone."

"I want to be," Brodie stated honestly. It would be so much easier.

His fingers touched her jaw, trailed down her neck. "I know you do, but that's not happening. Not this time."

Panic flooded her system and closed her throat. Wanting to protest, Brodie could only look at him with wide, scared eyes. She needed to push him away, to end the emotion swirling between them. "You just want to get into my pants again."

The only hint of Kade's frustration was the slight tightening of his fingers. She waited for him to retaliate but he just brushed his amused mouth in a hot kiss across her lips.

"So cynical, Brodie." He rubbed the cord in her neck with his thumb and Brodie couldn't miss the determination on his face and in the words that followed. "I want you, Brodie, you know that. But that is a completely separate matter to us raising a child together. One is about want and heat and crazy need, the other is about being your friend, a support structure, about raising this child together as best as we can."

"We can't be both friends and lovers, Kade!"

"We can be anything we damn well want," Kade replied. "But for now, why don't we try to be friends first and figure out how we're going to be parents and not complicate it with sex?"

He confused and bedazzled her, Brodie admitted. She couldn't keep up with him. She felt like she was being maneuvered into a corner, pushed there by the force of his will. "I don't know! I need to think."

Kade smiled, stepped back and placed his hands in the pockets of his khaki shorts. "You can think all you want, Brodie, but it isn't going to change a damn thing. I'm going to be around whether you like it or not." He ducked his head and dropped a kiss on her temple."You might as well get used to it," he murmured into her ear.

Before Brodie got her wits together to respond, Kade walked across the patio to the outside stairs. He snapped his fingers. Simon lumbered to his feet and they both jogged down the stairs. Brodie looked over the balustrade as they hit the ground below.

"And get some sleep, Stewart! You look like hell," Kade called.

Yeah, just what a girl needed to hear, Brodie thought. Then she yawned and agreed it was a very good suggestion.

Kade glanced down at his phone, the red flashing light indicating he had a message. He looked across the table to his friends and partners and saw they were still reading a condensed version of Logan's contract. He slid his finger across the screen and his breath hitched when he saw Brodie's name.

He hadn't spoken to her for two days but he kept seeing her in his mind's eye, looking down at him from the patio of the cabin—bemused, befuddled, so very tired. He had deliberately left her alone, wanting to give her time to get used to the idea of them co-parenting.

Back in the city. Thought that you might want to know.

Kade smiled at her caustic message. Not exactly gracious but coming from the independent Brodie, who'd rather cut off her right arm than ask for help, it was progress.

He quickly typed a reply.

Feeling rested?

A bit.

Any other symptoms?

Do you really want to know? He grimaced at the green, vomiting emoji tacked onto the end of the message.

Ugh. Will bring dinner. Around 7?

Tired. Going to bed early.

Oh, no. When was she going to learn that if she retreated he would follow? You have to eat. I'm bringing food. Be there.

Suit yourself.

That was Brodie speak for "see you later." Kade

tapped the screen and smiled. The trick with Brodie, he was learning, was to out-stubborn her.

"Kade, do you agree?"

"Sure," he murmured, looking straight through Quinn. He'd have to tell his friends at some point but there were reasons why he didn't want to, not yet. He was still wrapping his head around the situation and he wasn't ready for his friends to rag him about it. He still felt raw. The situation was uncertain and, consequently, his temper was quick to the boil.

Besides, it was one of those things he needed to discuss with Brodie… Was she ready for the pregnancy to become public knowledge?

He didn't think either of them was ready for the press. Especially since Brodie was supposed to be finding his dream woman. His next date. She was, after all, his damned matchmaker.

No, he definitely wasn't ready for the news to be splashed across the papers and social media. It was too new and too precious. Too fragile. Kade half turned and put his hand into the pocket of his suit jacket, which was hanging off the back of his chair. Pulling out a container of aspirin, he flipped back the lid and swallowed three, ignoring the bitter powder coating his mouth.

He'd had a low-grade headache since he'd left Brodie and he'd been popping aspirin like an addict. It was a small price to pay for a very large oops.

Kade looked up when he heard a knock on the

glass door. Two seconds later his personal assistant leaned into the room. "What's up, Joy?"

"There's someone here to see you and she's not budging," Joy told him after tossing a quick greeting to Quinn and Mac. Joy snapped her fingers. "Someone Stewart."

Kade frowned. Brodie? Was something wrong? She'd just been texting him. He stood up abruptly and his chair skittered backward. Crap! Something must be wrong. Brodie would never come to his office without calling first. He started toward the door and stopped when he saw the slight, stylish figure of Poppy Stewart walking toward them.

"Poppy? Is she okay?" He winced at the panic in his voice.

Poppy frowned. "Why wouldn't she be?" she said when she reached him. Kade placed a hand on his heart and sucked in a deep breath while Poppy graciously, but very firmly, sent Joy on her way. "We need to talk."

"You sure she's okay?"

"When I left she was eating an apple and drinking ginger tea. She has a slew of appointments today and was heading downtown later." Poppy walked into the conference room and Mac and Quinn rose to their feet.

"My, my, my," she crooned, holding out a delicate hand for them to shake, her mouth curved in a still sexy smile. "You boys certainly pack a punch."

Kade rubbed his forehead. God, he wasn't up to

dealing with a geriatric flirt. And why the hell wasn't the aspirin working?

"Poppy, why are you here?" he asked, dropping back into his chair.

Quinn pulled out a chair for Poppy and gestured for her to sit. "Can I offer you something to drink? Coffee? Tea?"

"I'm fine, thank you," Poppy replied.

Mac frowned at Kade. "I'm Mac McCaskill and this is Quinn Rayne."

God, he was losing his mind along with his manners. "Sorry, Poppy. Guys, this is Poppy Stewart."

"Stewart?" Quinn asked. "Any relation to Brodie Stewart, the matchmaker?"

"Great-aunt," Kade briefly explained. He caught his friends' eyes and jerked his head in the direction of the door.

Mac just sat down again and Quinn sat on the edge of the conference table. It would take a bomb to move them, Kade realized, so he stood up. "Let's go to my office, Poppy. We'll have some privacy there."

"You need privacy from your best friends?" Poppy asked.

Mac lifted an eyebrow. "Yeah, do you?"

"Right now, yeah!" Kade snapped. He rubbed his jaw before gripping the bridge of his nose with his finger and thumb.

"You haven't told them," Poppy said and he heard the amusement in her voice. Glad she was finding this funny because he sure as hell wasn't.

"Told us what?" Quinn asked, his eyes alight with curiosity.

Poppy's open hand drifted through the air, silently telling him it was his call whether to answer his friends or not. They had to know sometime. If he told them now, then he'd avoid them nagging him to distraction.

Kade looked toward the open door and crossed the floor, slamming it shut. They all knew the signal: closed door meant what was said in the room stayed in the room. Both Mac and Quinn nodded their agreement.

"Brodie is pregnant," Kade quietly said. He handed Mac a rueful smile. "I'm right behind you in the new-dads line."

Kade was grateful that beyond quietly congratulating him, Mac and Quinn didn't make a big song and dance over his announcement. Instead they just left the room, still looking shocked. All their lives were changing at a rapid pace. Just a few months ago they had been the most eligible bachelors in the city. Now Mac was getting married and he and Kade were both going to be fathers.

Then again, none of them ever eased their way into a situation, Kade thought as Mac shut the door behind him. They always jumped into the deep end and swam hard. "They took it rather well," Poppy said, linking her hands around her knee.

"They were behaving themselves in front of you,"

Kade explained. "Trust me, when they get me alone, they'll rip into me."

Kade dropped his head and rubbed the back of his neck. White-hot pain shot up his spine and bounced off the back of his skull. Hell, he hadn't had a migraine for years and, he recalled, they always started like this. It had been so long since an attack he'd stopped the habit of carrying medicine with him to take the edge off the pain.

"Are you unhappy about this baby, Kade?"

Kade had to concentrate hard for her words to make sense. "Not unhappy. Surprised, getting used to the idea. Wondering how we're going to make it work."

"You will," Poppy told him, sounding convinced. "And Brodie being pregnant is the reason I am here.

"I am scheduled to go on a cruise in a week or so. Ordinarily I would cancel the cruise and stay home with Brodie. I'm worried about her. But I am one of the tour leaders and they need me."

Kade held up a hand and silently cursed when he saw his vision was starting to double. Dammit, he had about fifteen minutes, a half hour at most, before he fell to the floor. "Do you want her to move in with me?"

"Not necessarily, but I am worried about her, Kade. She's sick and stressed and she's not sleeping, not eating. If no one keeps an eye on her, I worry I'll come back to a skeleton that swallowed a pea."

"How long are you away for?" God, it was getting difficult to concentrate.

"Two months. Are you okay? You look awfully pale."

That would be a negative. "I'll look after her… I'll keep an eye on her," Kade muttered, slurring his words.

"Oh, my God, you really don't look well. Can I call someone for you?"

He wanted to shrug off the pain, to act like nothing was wrong, but it felt like there were pickaxes penetrating his skull. "Call Mac, Quinn. Tell them… migraine."

"I'm on it." Poppy jumped up so fast the foot of her chair scraped along the floor and the sound sliced through Kade's head as he dropped his head to the desk.

When Brodie arrived at Kade's loft, Quinn opened the door to let her in. Brodie was surprised when he bent down and dropped a friendly kiss on her cheek. "Hey, pretty girl."

She couldn't feel offended. Quinn was so damn good-looking he could charm a fence post out of concrete. "Hey, Quinn." Brodie dropped her bag on the hall table and saw Mac standing by the floor-to-ceiling windows looking out at the incredible views of the city. "Hi, Mac."

"Hi, Brodie." He walked over to her and, equally surprisingly, dropped a kiss on her cheek.

"How is he?" she asked, biting her bottom lip.

"He's over the worst of it and this one was bad." Mac ran a hand through his hair.

"Does he get them often?" Brodie asked.

Quinn shook his head. "No, not anymore. He used to when he first joined the Mavericks but he hasn't had one for years."

"We think it's stress-induced," Mac quietly added. He looked at her stomach and back up to her eyes again and Brodie flushed. "He's got quite a bit to be stressed about at the moment."

"I told him he doesn't have to be! This is my problem. I can deal with it." Brodie felt sick and sad. It wasn't her fault Kade had endured two days of pain, that he'd been restricted to a darkened room, all because she'd told him she didn't need him.

She didn't need him.

"You don't know Kade at all if you think he'd just walk away from you and his child," Mac replied, ignoring her flash of temper. "And it's not only your situation causing his stress. He's dealing with a hell of a lot, work-wise, at the moment."

Brodie folded her arms across her chest and sucked in a calming breath. Mac was right; she didn't really know anything about Kade and she knew even less about what he dealt with on a daily basis.

Brodie looked down at the container of soup in her arms. She'd had a friend in college who suffered from migraines and she knew she battled to eat anything solid for days afterward. Chicken soup had been all her friend could stand. So, Brodie had whipped up a batch and decided to bring it over.

A little get-better-soon gesture from her baby's mommy to her baby's daddy. That was all that this visit was. All it could be. "Is he awake? Would he like something to eat?"

Quinn took the container from her and walked toward the kitchen. "He's still sleeping and likely to be asleep for another hour or two." Quinn exchanged a look with Mac and spoke again. "Hey, can you do us a favor?"

"Maybe," Brodie cautiously answered.

Quinn put down the container and placed his hands on the center island separating the dining area from the kitchen. "Can you hang out here for an hour or two and then wake Kade up and try to get him to eat?"

Mac nodded his agreement. "Our new player arrived in the city earlier this afternoon and the three of us were supposed to take him out to dinner. Quinn and I can still do that if you hang around here and feed Kade."

"Sure."

"We'll call you later and see how he's doing. If you think he's okay, then we'll go back to our own places."

"You've been here for two days?" Brodie asked, surprised.

Mac flushed. "We've taken shifts. He's a friggin' miserable patient and we could do with a break."

Kade had good friends, Brodie realized. Very good friends. There for each other through thick and thin. Brodie ignored her envy and nodded. "Go, I'll be fine."

"We know you will." Quinn walked up to her, placed his big hands on her shoulders. He gave her a slow, sweet, genuine smile. "Congratulations on the baby, Brodie. We can't wait to meet him…or her."

Brodie felt her throat tighten. "Thank you."

Quinn turned away and Mac bent down to give her a small hug. "Yeah, from me, too, Brodie. I don't know how you two are going to make this work but we're rooting for you. And Rory wants to have lunch. She says the two of you are reasonably smart people and you can figure out the pregnancy thing together."

"I'd like that," Brodie murmured.

Quinn pointed at the container. "Make him eat. He'll feel better for it."

Mac clapped Quinn on the shoulder and steered him to the door. "Stop fussing. Brodie can handle it."

"I know but he gets all depressed and mopey after a migraine," Quinn complained.

"Brodie. Will. Handle. It." With a last eye-roll at Brodie, Mac steered Quinn through the doors. He looked back and flashed Brodie a grin. "I swear after raising these two, having a kid is going to be a breeze."

Eight

"Go away, Quinn."

"Sorry, not Quinn." Brodie pushed open the door to Kade's bedroom and walked into the darkness to stand at the end of his bed. Her eyes adjusted and she took in his broad back, the yummy butt covered in a pair of loose boxers, the muscled thighs and calves. He was in great shape—long, lean and muscular. Powerful.

"Brodie?" Kade rolled over and leaned on one elbow. He pushed his hair back from his forehead and squinted at her. "What are you doing here?"

Brodie clasped her hands behind her back. "I brought you some chicken soup and your buds asked me to check on you to see if you're not, well, dead."

"They'd be so lucky," Kade growled, sitting up and resting his elbows on his bent knees.

"How are you feeling?"

"Horrible."

"That good, huh?"

Kade lifted a muscular shoulder. "It's a combination of relief that the pain is gone and mental exhaustion. My head is sore."

"Do you still have headache?"

"Not a migraine…" Kade tried to explain. "It's more like my brain is tired. For a day afterward I feel exhausted, like I have a mental hangover."

"Are you sure you're not pregnant? Add nausea and vomiting and that's how I feel all the time."

"Sorry, babe." Kade patted the mattress next to him. "What are you doing over there? Come here."

She really shouldn't. If she sat down next to him she wouldn't be able to keep her hands to herself and then she'd get naked and he had a headache. And he needed to date other women—women she'd found for him!—and she was supposed to be keeping a mental and emotional distance so there were like, a hundred reasons why she shouldn't sit down, why she shouldn't even be here…

Despite all that, Brodie walked around the bed to sit on its edge. Kade immediately wound an arm around her waist, pulled her backward and spooned her from behind. His hand covered her breast and she sighed. "Kade…"

"Shhh." Kade touched his lips to her neck and

thumbed her nipple. It bloomed under his touch and she felt heat rushing down, creating a fireball between her legs.

"I need you," Kade whispered in her ear. "I need to be inside you, touching you, being with you. Say yes, Brodes."

Brodie rolled over to face him and touched his jaw, his lips. She opened her mouth to speak but Kade placed his fingers over her lips. "I don't want to hear that this is a bad idea, that we shouldn't, that this is madness. I know it is and, right now, *I don't care.*"

Oh, in all honesty, she didn't, either. Wasn't she allowed to step away from the complications and just enjoy his touch, take pleasure in the way he made her feel? Making love to Kade was sheer bliss and, after the weeks she'd endured, wasn't she entitled to some fun? To escape for a little while? It didn't have to mean anything. She wanted him, needed him—in her, filling her, completing her.

"You have too many clothes on, babe." Kade covered her breast with one hand. She arched into his hand, frustrated at the barriers between him and her skin.

"I'm happy for you to take them off as quickly as you can," Brodie whispered, curling her hand around the back of his neck.

"Then again, I rather like you like this. All flushed and hot and horny."

Brodie whimpered when Kade's hard mouth dropped over hers and his tongue tangled with hers.

He used his arm to yank her on top of him and her thighs slid over his hips so she was flush against his erection, the heat of which she felt through her loose cotton trousers. His mouth teased and tormented hers—one minute his kisses were demanding and dominating, then he'd ease away. Lust whipped through her as she angled her head to allow him deeper access. His kisses seemed different from anything they'd shared before…there was more heat, more desire, more…of something indefinable.

Unsettled but still incredibly eager, Brodie gripped his shoulders as he undid the buttons on her shirt and exposed her lace-covered breasts to his intense gaze. Kade used one finger to pull down the lace cup and expose her puckered nipple. Then his tongue licked her and sensations swamped her. She moaned when he flicked open the tiny clasp holding her bra together and revealed her torso to his exploring hand. He pulled aside the pale yellow fabric of her bra and swiped his thumb across her peaked nipple. She arched her back, silently asking for more. Kade lowered his head and took one puckered nipple into his mouth, his tongue sliding over her, hot and wet. Kade heard her silent plea for him to touch her and his hand moved to her hip, pushing underneath the waist of her trousers.

"Lift up," he muttered and Brodie lifted her hips and straightened her legs, allowing him to push the fabric down her thighs.

Kade tapped her bottom. "Move off for a sec."

She rolled away and he whipped off his boxers. He put his hands on her knees and pulled them apart before dragging his finger over her mound, slipping under the fabric to find her wet and wanting.

"I want you so much."

"Then *take* me." Really, did the man need a gilded invitation?

Kade sent her a wicked smile. "Yeah, in a minute."

"How's your head?"

Kade looked down and lifted an eyebrow. "Just fine and eager to say hi."

Brodie laughed and slapped his shoulder. "Your other head!"

"Also fine."

Brodie rubbed her thumb against the two grooves between his eyebrows. "Liar. Do you want to stop?"

Brodie hissed as two fingers slipped into her passage.

"Do I look like I want to stop?"

"Kade!" She reached for him, fumbling in her eagerness to get him inside her. "Please, just… I want you."

"I want you this way first. I want to watch you come, with my fingers inside you and my mouth kissing yours." Kade lifted his head and looked into her eyes. "You look good like this, Brodie. You look good anywhere, anyhow."

She was so close, teetering on the edge. *"Kade!"*

"You take my breath away when you lose yourself

in me, in the way I make you feel. How do I make you feel, Brodie?"

He was expecting her to speak, to think? How could she answer when she felt like she was surfing a white-hot band of pure, crazy sensation?

"Tell me, Brodie."

"Free," Brodie gasped. "Safe. Sexy."

Cherished, Brodie silently added as her climax rocked her. All those wonderful, loved-up, fuzzy emotions she had no business experiencing. Brodie cried out, partly in reckless abandon and partly in pain as her heart swelled and cracked the plaster she'd cast around it.

She was being wild but she didn't care. She'd deal with the consequences, and the pain, later. Right now she just wanted to feel.

She wanted to feel alive. Just for a little while.

Brodie had to open various cupboard doors before she found soup bowls and three drawers before she found a ladle. She placed a bowl of soup in the microwave to heat and while it did its thing, she scratched around until she found place mats and flatware.

Brodie looked up as Kade entered the kitchen and her breath caught in the back of her throat. Kade looked shattered but somehow, just dressed in a pair of straight-legged track pants and a plain red T-shirt, hot. His hair was damp from his shower and his stubble glinted in the bright light of the kitchen.

Kade frowned and walked over to a panel on the

wall and dimmed the lights. "Better," he muttered. He walked back to the island and pulled out a bar stool and sat down.

The microwave dinged. Brodie grabbed a dish towel and pulled out the hot bowl of soup. She put it onto the place mat and pushed the mat, a spoon and the bowl in Kade's direction.

He wrinkled his nose. "I appreciate the offer but I don't think I can eat."

"Listen, Quinn—who, surprisingly, is a fusser—will call and I need to tell him you ate or else he is going to come over here and make you eat." Brodie dished some soup for herself. "And frankly, tonight I think he could make you. You look about as tough as overboiled noodles."

"Thanks."

"At least I didn't say you look like hell." Brodie pointed her spoon at him.

Kade winced. "Sorry, but you did. You are looking better. Still tired, but better."

"I've been living on chicken soup." Brodie sat down and nodded at his bowl. "It's good, try it."

Kade dipped his spoon, lifted it to his mouth and Brodie waited. When he smiled slowly and nodded she knew he approved. "It's my mom's recipe. A cure for all ailments." And, years later, still doing its job.

They ate in comfortable silence until Brodie looked around the loft and sighed. "My dad was a builder. He would've loved this place."

"You sound uncomfortable when you talk about your parents," he said. "Why?"

Because she was, because she felt guilt that they'd died and she didn't. Because she still missed them with every breath she took. Kade waited for her explanation and, despite her tight throat, she told him what she was thinking. "It's just hard," she concluded.

"You're lucky you experienced such love, such acceptance. They sound like they were incredibly good parents."

Brodie pushed away her plate, looking for an excuse not to talk. But she couldn't keep doing that, not if they were going to co-parent. She needed to learn to open up, just a little. "They were. I was the center of their universe, the reason the sun came up for them every morning." She rested her chin in the palm of her hand. "That makes me sound like I was spoiled, but I wasn't, not really. They gave me more experiences than things. They gave me attention and time, and, most importantly, roots and wings. I felt… lost when they died. I still feel lost," Brodie admitted. "And so damn scared."

Kade took one more sip of soup before standing up. He picked up the bowls and carried them to the sink, leaving them there. On his return trip, he stopped at Brodie's chair and held out his hand. "Let's go sit."

Brodie put her hand in his and followed him across the room to the mammoth sofa. Kade sat down and pulled Brodie next to him, placing his hand on her knee to keep her there. They looked at the city lights and Brodie finally allowed her head to drop so her temple rested on Kade's shoulder.

"What scares you, Brodie?"

Brodie heard his quiet question and sighed. "Love scares me. Feeling attached and running the risk of losing the person I am attached to scares me. Being a mommy scares the pants off me."

"Why?"

"I know how quickly life can change. One day I was bright, happy and invincible. The next I'd lost everyone that mattered to me." She had to continue; she couldn't stop now. "I not only lost my parents in a single swoop, but my two best friends, too. I survived the accident with minor physical injuries and major emotional ones."

He didn't mutter meaningless words of sympathy. He just put her onto his lap, his arms holding her against his broad chest.

Him holding her was all she needed.

"Tell me about your childhood," she asked, desperate to change the subject.

Kade stared out the window at the breathtaking views of False Creek and the city. Brodie wondered if he ever got used to it. Kade, reading her mind, gestured to the window. "I do my best thinking here, looking out of this window. It's never the same, always different depending on the time of day, the month, the season. It's a reminder that nothing stays the same. As a kid my life was nothing *but* change."

Brodie half turned so she could watch his face as he talked. This was the first time they'd dropped some of their barriers and it was frightening. This was something she'd done with her friends, with Chels and Jay. She was out of practice.

"After my mom died, my dad packed up our house, sold everything and hit the road. He wanted to see the country. He wanted to paint. He couldn't leave me behind and he wouldn't stay so I went along. I went to many, many different schools. Some for months, some for only weeks. In some places I didn't even get to school. My education was—" Kade hesitated "—sporadic."

Brodie knew if she spoke she'd lose him so she just waited for him to continue talking.

"But while I hated school, I loved to play hockey and I could always make friends on the ice. Especially since I was good and everyone wanted me on their team. But invariably I'd find a team, make some friends, start to feel settled and he'd yank me off to someplace new."

"I'm sorry."

"So in a way we're the same, Brodie."

Brodie frowned, unsure of where he was going with this. "How?"

"You're scared to become emotionally involved because you're scared to lose again. I'm scared for the same reason." Kade dropped his hand to pat her stomach. "We're going to have to find a way to deal with those fears because this little guy—"

"It could be a girl."

Kade's smile was soft and sweet. "This baby is going to need us, what we can give her. Or him. Individually or together."

His words were low and convincing and Brodie finally accepted he wasn't going to change his mind about the baby. He was determined to play his part parenting their child. Okay then, that was something she would have to get used to.

So, how did they deal with their attraction while they learned to navigate the parenting landscape?

"Problem?"

Brodie wiggled her butt against his long length and heard his tortured hiss. "The fact that we are stupidly attracted to each other is a problem."

"It is?"

"I am not falling into a relationship with you just because we are going to be co-parents, Kade."

A small frown pulled his strong eyebrows together. "Were we talking about a relationship?"

"I just… We just…" Dammit, he made her sound like a blithering idiot.

"Relax, Brodie." He touched her lips, her jaw. "I want you, just like I wanted you forty-five minutes ago, last week, six weeks ago. Not because of the baby but because you drain the blood from my brain. It's a totally separate issue from us being parents. We can do it."

"I don't see how."

"That's because you could complicate a three-piece jigsaw puzzle," Kade teased. "So we slept together again…"

"Yeah, we weren't supposed to do that."

The corners of Kade's mouth tipped up in amusement. "On, the plus side, at least we know you won't fall pregnant."

"Ha-ha." Brodie stared at his broad chest. "I still think we should try to be friends. Our lives are complicated enough already without dealing with sex."

"Why can't we be friends who make love?"

"Because it never works. What if you meet someone you like, someone you desire more than me? I still have to find you two more dates. What if you fall head over heels in love with one of them?"

Kade's hand on her thigh tightened and then relaxed. "What if the sky fell down in the morning?" he drawled. "Do you always borrow trouble like this?"

Her sky had fallen down and trouble had landed on her door. She just wanted to protect herself from it happening again. Was that so wrong? Talking to him, opening up, was dangerous. If she wasn't careful she could love him. She couldn't—wouldn't—allow herself to do that.

Brodie started to move away, to climb off his lap, to find some physical and emotional distance, but his arms held her close.

"No, don't go, Brodes. Just rest that brain of yours, take some time to regroup. Stop thinking."

It was such a huge temptation to rest a while in his embrace. Surrounded by him she felt like nothing could hurt her, that the world and her life weren't quite as scary as she imagined them to be.

"Just rest, sweetheart. We'll figure it out, I promise." Kade's deep voice sounded almost tender. Brodie curled into him and placed her cheek on his chest, her ear directly over his heart. If she closed her eyes she would just drift off...

Brodie rolled over onto her stomach and looked across the coffee table. It was a beautiful day and the sky was a bright, clear blue. Beyond False Creek the Pacific Ocean looked grumpy and the wind teased the water, creating white horses on its surface. If she ignored the morning sickness, she felt better than she had for days, maybe weeks.

Last night, instead of thinking, planning, shoring up her defenses, instead of arguing, she'd allowed Kade to pull her head back to his chest and loop his arms around her. His hand, drawing lazy circles on her back, had lulled her to sleep. She had a vague memory of him picking her up and placing her on the large couch and wrapping his long body around hers as she slept. He'd kept her restless dreams at bay and the feeling of being protected, cared for, had allowed her to drop into a deep, rejuvenating sleep.

Brodie sat up and pushed her hair out of her eyes.

She looked over her shoulder and saw Kade standing at the center island, watching her. Something deep, hot and indefinable sparked between them and Brodie bit her bottom lip. Sexy, rumpled man, she thought. How was she supposed to resist him?

"Come here, Brodie," Kade said, his voice as deep and dark as his gaze, the order in it unmistakable.

She knew what would follow if she stood up. She heard it in his voice, saw it in the desire flashing in his eyes, in the way he gripped the counter, tension rippling through his arms. He wanted her…

Brodie knew she shouldn't, knew this was a mistake but she stood up anyway. On shaky legs, she crossed the space to the kitchen, walked around the island and stopped a foot away from him. Seeing a half-empty glass of orange juice, she picked it up and took a long sip. Excitement and desire caused her hand to shake and orange juice ran down her chin.

Kade wiped the droplets off with his thumb. "I have to kiss you."

Brodie started to speak but Kade shook his head. "No, don't say it's a mistake, that we shouldn't be doing this. Just forget about everything else. This is just about you and me… There are no other complications right now. They'll be back later, but right now…? There's nothing but you…and me."

"I was just going to tell you to hurry up," Brodie whispered, lifting her face. "Hurry up and kiss me, Kade."

Kade leaned forward, cupped the side of her face

in his hand and lowered his mouth to hers. Part of her thought that if Kade did nothing else but kiss her for the rest of her life, she could die happy. Another section of her brain just squawked warnings: they had to be friends only. She still had to be his matchmaker. They shouldn't be doing this. If the media found out they would go nuts. Then Kade took control of her mouth, her brain shut down and she felt energized, revitalized, as if he'd plugged her in to recharge.

"Take me to bed, Kade," she muttered against his lips as her arms looped around his neck and her fingers played with the taut skin there.

Kade groaned. "Yeah, that was my intention. Except that my bed is too far." Kade used his forearm to push everything standing on the center island to the far edge of the block before bending his knees and wrapping one arm around her hips. In one easy, fluid movement he had her sitting on the island, their hands and mouths now perfectly aligned. Brodie placed her palms on Kade's shoulders and tipped her head to give him better access so he could brush his lips against her neck, her jaw, her cheekbones.

"You are so beautiful."

She wasn't, not really, but right now she believed him. Feeling sexy and confident, she dropped her hands and gripped his T-shirt, slowly pulling it up and over his chest, wanting to get her hands on those muscles. Kade used one hand to finish pulling the T-shirt over his head and toss it to the floor. Brodie sucked in her breath. His track pants were low on his hips, displaying his ripped abdomen, those long obliques over his hips. Those sexy muscles made her feel squirmy and stupid and so, so wanton.

Brodie's fingers drifted over his abdomen and hips, the side of her hand brushing his erection. She heard Kade suck in a breath. Liking the fact that she could make him breathe faster, that she could make his eyes glaze over, she pushed her hands inside his pants and pushed them over his hips to fall into a black puddle on the wooden floor.

"Whoops." She smiled against his mouth.

"Since the urge to strip is all I ever think about when you are in the room, I'm not complaining," Kade said, his mouth curling into a delighted smile.

His smile could melt ice cream, make women walk into poles and stop traffic. It heated up every one of Brodie's internal organs and made them smile, too.

He had a hell of a smile, Brodie thought, especially when she felt it on her skin.

Nine

A few days later, Brodie parked her car next to Kade's and ran an appreciative hand over the sleek hood. Had Kade realized this car was something he'd have to give up or, at the very least, that he'd need to buy a new one to transport the baby? There was no room for a car seat and she doubted a stroller would fit in the trunk.

So much was changing, Brodie thought as she headed to the entrance of his apartment building, quickly keying in the code to open the front doors. She and Kade were sort of lovers, kind of friends, about to be parents. The parenting bit was the only thing she was certain of, she thought as she walked into the private elevator that opened into Kade's hallway.

Kade could rocket her from zero to turned-on in two seconds flat. And he was funny and smart… She was crazy about him.

Brodie rested her head against the panel of the elevator, petrified she was building castles in the air. She was pregnant and it was so natural to look to the father of her baby for sex, for comfort. It made complete sense. Who wanted to be a single parent, who wanted to go through this frightening, exhausting, terrifying process alone? But castles built on fantastic sex and thin air and wishes could collapse at a moment's notice. Kade wasn't going to be her happily-ever-after guy. She didn't believe in happily-ever-after. She believed in getting through, doing the best she could, building a safe and secure life. There was only one person she could rely on 100 percent and that was herself.

Brodie hit the emergency stop button and rested her forehead against the elevator door. She had to pull back from him, had to put some distance between them. She was being seduced by what-ifs and how-it-might-be's. She couldn't afford to think of Kade as anything more than the father of her child. He was her temporary lover but he wasn't her partner or her significant other.

He *definitely* would never be her husband.

The last time she'd planned her future she'd had it ripped from her. She'd lost everyone she'd loved in one fell swoop and she refused to take that risk again.

She couldn't taste love, hold love and lose love again. That was too big a risk to take.

She smacked the emergency button and the elevator lurched upward.

No, she'd had her fun…too much fun. It was time to back the hell away and get a handle on this relationship. She needed to dial it back to a cordial friendship. She could do that. And she *would* do that before the story broke in the press. Presently the press saw her as nothing more than his matchmaker but they'd soon sniff out the truth. With her spending nights at his place, they'd been lucky to keep it a secret this long.

Luck, as she knew, always ran out.

Kade walked into his loft, ignored Mac and Rory and Quinn, and walked straight over to Brodie. He picked her up and turned her upside down so her head was facing the floor. She gurgled with laughter and placed her hands on the floor to steady herself.

"Kade, she's pregnant!" Quinn grabbed his arm. "What are you doing?"

"I'm getting blood to her head, something that was obviously missing when she chose my date," Kade replied, easily restoring Brodie to her feet. "She's lucky I didn't hang her over the balcony."

Brodie wiped her hands on the seat of her pants and sent him a cocky smile. She hadn't been remotely scared at being tossed around like a doll,

Kade mused. Her eyes were bright and full of mischief. “Really, Stewart?”

Brodie attempted an innocent shrug. “What? She’s a biokinetics engineer and a part-time entertainer.”

“And a full-time loony. She wants to be a freakin’ mermaid.” Kade pointed an accusing finger at Brodie.

“What are we talking about?” Mac asked, mystified.

“The latest date Brodie and Wren sent him on. He had lunch with her today,” Quinn explained. He turned to Kade. “You do know it’s weird that you’re going on these dates while Brodie is pregnant with your child?”

No, the thought hadn’t occurred to him, he sarcastically, silently replied. Brodie and he had an understanding—basically, they both understood they had no idea what they were doing. “Blame Wren. Besides, the dating is done.”

“When did you do date number two?” Mac asked.

“A couple of weeks back. Teacher, triathlete. We had lunch,” Kade answered him. “I am now off the dating hook.”

“Anyway, getting back to today and this date—” he pointed a finger at Brodie “—revenge will be sweet.”

Brodie didn’t seem particularly concerned, so Kade left her to talk to his friends and headed for the kitchen. On the plus side, he’d fulfilled his duties to Wren’s publicity campaign. The public could vote, speculate and talk about his love life until the damn cows came home but the only woman who interested him, on any level, was standing on his balcony, carrying his child.

He opened the fridge, yanked out a beer, saw Quinn behind him and reached for another. Kade handed Quinn a bottle and closed the fridge door with a nudge of his knee. He cracked open the beer and took a long swallow. He looked across the loft to the balcony where Brodie stood. It was a nice evening, his friends were here and he'd ordered Thai for dinner. He'd had a busy, drama-free day and then he'd joined Quinn and Mac on the ice for a workout. While the news had been unexpected, he was going to be a father and he was starting to become excited at the prospect.

Life *should* be good.

So what was the problem? In a nutshell, it was this half on, half off, up-in-the-air arrangement he had with Brodie. Half friends, sometimes lovers, future parents, both of them wanting, on some level, to run. He was jogging in place but Brodie had her sneakers on and was about to sprint, as hard and as fast as she could.

As soon as she could.

Kade felt he was living the same life he'd lived with his father, not sure how the next move would affect him. Every day was new territory for him and he felt as unsettled as he had when he was a child.

Quinn's fist smacking into Kade's biceps rocked

him back to the here and now. "What the hell was that for?"

"I talk to both you and Mac but neither of you listen! It's like talking to a blow-up doll."

"You should know," Kade grumbled, rubbing his arm.

Quinn's fist shot out again but Kade stepped back and the fist plowed through air. Kade sent Quinn a mocking glance. "Too slow, bro."

Quinn picked up his beer bottle, sipped and after lowering it he spoke again. "You concentrating, dude?"

"Yeah." Kade leaned against the kitchen counter and crossed his legs. "Speak."

"Your dad is having an exhibition in a couple of weeks, downtown."

So? His father was a well-respected artist and frequently held exhibitions in the city. James didn't invite him to any and Kade didn't attend. It worked for both of them. "Not interested."

"The exhibition is called 'Retrospective Regrets.'"

Kade didn't give a crap. His father wasn't part of his life, hadn't been part of his life for a long, long time. And he liked it that way.

"I just thought you might like to tell him he's going to be a grandfather."

He hadn't wanted a son so Kade doubted he'd be interested in a grandchild. But maybe he should give James the benefit of the doubt? Maybe he'd changed. Kade cursed at the hope that flickered.

"I'll think about it."

Quinn knew better than to push. He just shrugged and lifted his beer bottle in Brodie's direction. "What are you going to do about her? Are you going to marry her, live with her, demand joint custody?"

Kade wished he knew. "I definitely want joint custody, everything else is up in the air." He rested his beer bottle against his forehead and sighed. "It's all craziness."

"Well, I suggest you figure out what you are before the news of your impending fatherhood hits the papers. If you don't know they'll decide for you."

Because the media's focus had been on his dates and the future of the team, so far he and Brodie had managed to dodge that bullet, but Kade wasn't under any illusions they'd keep the baby a secret indefinitely.

Quinn grinned. "On the plus side, my BASE jumping and having to talk myself out of being arrested aren't quite so bad when you measure them against the fact that another Maverick-teer is going to become a father, barely a month after Mac."

Kade would cross that burning bridge when he came to it. And talking about daredevil stunts… "Talking of, are you insane? You could've been killed!"

"Only if my chute didn't open," Quinn cheerfully agreed. "Then I would've made a dent in the concrete. *Splat!*"

Kade sent Brodie an anxious look, grateful she hadn't heard Quinn's cavalier attitude toward death.

"Not funny, Rayne." Kade stopped, whirled around and slapped his hand on Quinn's hard chest. He scowled at his best friend. "Brodie lost everyone she loved in one accident. Don't you dare be glib about death, yours or anyone else's, around her! Got it?"

Quinn rubbed the spot on his chest. "Jeez, okay! Got it."

Kade walked away and Quinn scowled at the ceiling.

"I'm running out of friends to play with," he muttered.

Later in the week, after a night long on pleasure and short on sleep, Brodie stood at the center island in Kade's kitchen, and scowled at her daily calendar on her tablet screen. Her schedule was utterly insane and she would be rushing from one appointment to another, all with men looking for a happily-ever-after. Didn't they realize the closer and the more perfect the relationship, the more pain they could expect to feel if the relationship went south? The end always hurt the most when the connection felt the best. Argh...she normally never thought about how her clients progressed after she matched them. Damn this situation with Kade for making her so introspective!

Kade, on his way up from the gym, walked past her to the sink and filled a glass with water. He whistled when he caught a glimpse of her schedule. "And I thought I had a hectic day ahead."

"Crazy, isn't it?" Brodie sipped her coffee and

scowled at the screen. "I won't take all these men on as clients, some I'll be able to help and some I'll discard because, well, they'll be idiots."

Kade rested the glass on his folded arm. "Why matchmaking, Brodie? Why earn your living from something you don't believe in?"

Why would he think that? "But I do believe in it. I do believe people function best when they are in healthy, stable, supportive relationships. Being alone sucks."

"But you avoid relationships. You are alone," Kade pointed out.

"Yeah, but that's the choice I've made." Brodie picked up a banana from the fruit bowl and slowly peeled it. "I know it's ironic that I, commitment-phobic as I am, own a matchmaking service."

Kade put his hands behind him and gripped the counter. "Okay, so why do you?"

Brodie looked across the loft to the rainy day outside. She took a bite of the banana, chewed it slowly and then placed it on the side plate next to her half-eaten toast. Should she tell Kade? Was she brave enough to open up a little more? She rarely—okay, never—spoke about Jay. She had trained herself not to think about him. But Kade was the father of her baby and she almost trusted him. Well, as much as she could.

"In the car crash, I didn't only lose my parents, I lost my best friends, as well. Chelsea and Jay. We were all in the car. I survived, and they didn't. We were like you and Mac and Quinn—inseparable."

Brodie swiped her finger across the program to close her calendar. "Jay and I always knew that, one day, we'd move on from being best friends. Three weeks before the crash, we finally admitted we loved each other. We started sleeping together, everything was new and bright and wonderful." Her voice cracked and Brodie cleared her throat.

Kade took a step forward but Brodie held up her hand to stop him. If he touched her she would start to cry and she had clients to see. "I lost my world in the space of three minutes. But I was so loved, Kade. So damn much."

"And you don't want that again?"

"I can't *lose* that again. I'll have this child and that'll be enough. This child arrived by sheer fluke and I've accepted that the baby is life's way of forcing me to love again. To love in a different way."

"And will that be enough?"

Brodie lifted one shoulder in a tiny shrug. "It has to be. It's all I'm prepared to risk." Her smile felt a little shaky. "I am going to be the best mother I can be. I am going to be your friend, your lover, for as long as that works or until you meet the woman you can't live without." Brodie rubbed her hands across her eyes. "I hope you find her, Kade. I'd like you to. I think you deserve her."

"And I think you deserve the same."

"I wouldn't be that lucky, not twice. Life doesn't work that way." Brodie pushed her tablet into its case and sighed. "I have to go. Busy day."

"It's barely seven, Brodie, and I need to talk to you about something else."

Brodie frowned at his tone. Being bossed around so early in the morning really didn't work for her. "Okay, what?"

"So gracious." Kade walked across the kitchen to take a mug from a shelf. He jammed it under the spout of his coffee machine and pushed a button. Brodie tapped her fingers against the counter, listening to the sounds of the beans grinding. She was feeling exposed and hot, like her skin was a size too small for her body. That's why she didn't usually talk, she reminded herself. It made her feel sad and funny and…weird.

"I'm going to need to tell the press something about us and soon."

"Why?"

Kade looked at her over the rim of his mug. "We spend a lot of time together and someone is going to realize that. And when you start showing, they'll go into overdrive. Wren suggests we hit them with a press release and cut off the speculation. So what do you want to be called? My girlfriend, my partner, my common-law wife?"

Brodie grimaced as he said the word *wife* and Kade scratched his head. "Okay, so not wife. What?"

This was far too much to deal with so early in the morning. "I don't like titles. I don't believe in them. We are what we are…"

"I'll just tell the press that. It'll work," Kade said, sounding sarcastic.

"I don't know, Kade!" Brodie cried. "Tell them we are friends, that we intend to remain friends, that we are having a baby together! That's all the information they are entitled to. That's all the information we have."

"They'll make it up if we don't give them more. Or they'll dig and dig until they find more," Kade warned.

She couldn't control their actions, Brodie thought. She could only control her own. And right now she had to get to work or else she'd be late for her breakfast appointment. Besides, she really didn't want to talk about this anymore. With Kade or the world. "I'm not ready to say anything yet. And I've got to go."

"Dammit, Brodie! We have to deal with this at some point."

Yeah, but not now.

"Think about it," Kade told her, obviously frustrated. "Are you coming back here tonight?"

Brodie slung her bag over her shoulder and walked toward the front door feeling hemmed in. "Maybe."

That one word was, right now, all she could commit to.

Brodie looked up when Colin tapped on the frame of her door and ambled into her office.

"Hey, Col." Brodie rested her forearms on her desk and sent him a fond smile.

"How are you feeling?"

"I'm well. The morning sickness has passed, as has the tiredness." Brodie bit her bottom lip. "Did you tell Kayla?"

A shadow passed through Colin's eyes as he nodded. Colin and Kayla had been trying to get pregnant for more than five years and were now trying IVF. Hearing Brodie had become pregnant via a one-night stand had probably rocked Kayla.

"She took it rather well, considering. She said to tell you she wants to meet the baby's daddy."

Yeah, about that. Brodie still hadn't told Colin, or anyone else, about Kade.

"Maybe," Brodie hedged.

Colin sighed. "You're going to keep us guessing, aren't you?"

Brodie rubbed her forehead with her fingertips. "It's complicated. We're trying to work through it and until we have a plan, I'd rather just keep his identity quiet." She wrinkled her nose. "I might end up parenting on my own and he won't be a factor."

Not that there was a snowball's chance in hell of that happening. This was, after all, Kade she was talking about.

"Understood," Colin said, before straightening. "So, business..."

Business talk she could do. Mostly because it stopped her thinking about Kade and their future. Business wasn't complicated or demanding and it didn't mess with her head. Or her libido. "What's up?"

"I don't know about you but I am overwhelmed. My schedule is crazy."

Brodie looked at her screen and the thirty unopened emails from prospective clients. Ironically, the publicity generated from being Kade's matchmaker had generated almost too much business. "It's crazy."

"I was approached by a couple out of Los Angeles who want to relocate to Vancouver. They have a matchmaking business in the city." Colin passed her a black-and-pink business card.

"I know the Hendersons," Brodie said, flicking her nail against the card. "I investigated their business model when I was starting this business. They are reputable, smart and sensitive."

"Well, they have just sold their business and they are moving here."

Brodie immediately connected the dots. "Are they going to start up here?"

"They want to semi-retire. They want to work but they don't want the responsibility of running an office or staff."

"Are you thinking about bringing them on board…with you?"

Colin picked up her pen and tapped it against his knee, leaving tiny blue dots on his khaki pants. "And with you, if you are as overwhelmed as I am. It's a win-win situation. We feed them clients, take a commission and we manage how big a bite they take."

Brodie looked at the pile of folders on her desk

and realized it might be the answer to her crazy workload. And she'd find it easier to juggle her career and being a new mother if she had some help. "Are they keen?"

"They are keen to talk," Colin replied. "They'll fly out here if we ask them to."

Her phone chirped and Brodie looked down at the screen.

Will be home late. Will you be okay?

God, she'd been okay for the past three months and for nine years before that. She'd managed to feed herself, dress herself, get herself to work, establish a career. Why did Kade and Poppy think she had dropped sixty IQ points just because she was now pregnant?

Arrrgh.

Brodie ignored Kade's message, pushed back her chair and stood up. She gripped the back of the chair.

"Or we could go to them." God, a trip out of the city would be an unexpected blessing, Brodie thought. She could get some distance from Kade, have some time alone to think.

You just don't want to deal with the emotions Kade pulls to the surface.

I just want some time to think! Is that too much to ask?

You've got to stop lying to yourself...

Oh, shut up.

Brodie looked at Colin. "What do you think? You up for a trip?"

"Sure. Are you allowed to fly?"

Brodie tamped down her irritation. "I am only a few months pregnant. The baby is the size of pea so yes, I can fly. Jeez!"

Her phone beeped again. I can cancel dinner if you want me to.

Kade! Really? She tipped her head at Colin and sent him an I-dare-you look. "Let's fly out tonight, see the Hendersons in the morning? I might stay in Cali for the weekend, do some sightseeing, some shopping."

Colin jumped to his feet, nodding enthusiastically. He was always up for an adventure and was, thank goodness, impulsive. "That sounds like an excellent idea. I'll call the Hendersons. Can you book flights?"

She could and she would, she thought, glancing down at the screen of her phone. Because she *definitely* needed to put a border and a couple of cities between her and Kade Webb.

Ten

Kade couldn't remember when he'd been this angry. Angry, disappointed…hurt, dammit. And the fact he was hurt pissed him off even more.

Gone away. Will be back in a few days.

A few days had turned into a week and he still didn't know where the hell Brodie was and, crucially, whether she was all right. She was ducking his calls and not returning his increasingly irate text messages. His…whatever the hell she was…was AWOL and he was not amused. Not amused as in ready to slam his fist into the wall. He'd do it but he recalled, from previous experience, it hurt like a bitch.

Kade stood on the balcony off his master suite and gripped the edge of the balustrade, peering past the trees to the street below, hoping to see Brodie's car. He wanted to make sure she was okay, to make love to her, to put her over his knee and spank her silly for driving him out of his mind with worry.

What if she never came back? What if she'd just packed up and left town, heading for…wherever? What would he do? How would he find her? Would he make the effort to track her down?

Of course he would. Apart from the fact she drove him insane, she was the mother of his child. For that reason alone he'd follow her to the ends of the earth…

Jesus, Brodie, where the hell are you?

Kade heard the subdued chime signaling someone had accessed his private elevator and since Quinn was out of town and Mac was home with Rory, it had to be Brodie. *Thank God.* She was the only other person who had the code.

Kade waited for the elevator doors to open and his heart both stumbled and settled when she stepped into his loft. He did a quick scan, confirmed she was physically in one piece and told himself not to lose his temper.

Yeah, that wasn't going to happen.

Brodie only needed one look to see Kade was pissed and exceptionally so. His eyes were the color of bittersweet chocolate and flat with anger and residual worry. She'd needed time away but she'd been wrong to avoid his calls, to avoid talking to him.

She'd done him a disservice; Kade was a fully functioning adult and he would've understood her need for some time alone to think. But she'd been unable to pick up the phone and tell him that—due to embarrassment and pride. Instead she'd let him worry and, judging by the increasingly irate messages he'd left her, stew. She deserved the verbal slap she was about to get and she braced herself to take it.

She'd created this situation and she wasn't going to whine about the consequences. She'd acted like a child because she'd felt smothered, and she deserved to be treated like a child now that she'd returned. He'd yell and she'd apologize and hopefully it would all be over soon.

"Hey."

Kade frowned and started to walk in her direction. Ah, hell, he was even angrier than she realized. Brodie lifted up her hands in apology. "I'm so—"

Her words were cut off by his hot mouth on hers and she could taste his frustration. His fingers dug into her hips and he yanked her into him, slamming her against his hard frame and his even harder erection. She couldn't help it; she encircled her arms around his neck and poured her own frustrations into the kiss…

I want you but I don't want to rely on you. I like feeling protected and cared for but it scares me spit-

less. I'm so close to falling in love with you but I can't let myself be that vulnerable again.

Brodie felt Kade tugging her shirt from her jeans and sighed when his warm hands spanned her back. His thigh pushed between hers and suddenly she was straddling his hard leg. Her body responded immediately by rocking against those hard muscles, moaning when the friction caught her in exactly the right place. Kade immediately responded by slipping his hand down the back of her jeans and he growled when her tight pants stopped his progress.

"Get them off."

This was too intense, too urgent, and Brodie knew they should back off, but she didn't want to. She wanted him out of control and reckless, demanding and insistent. He was feeling raw and so was she. It added an edge of excitement she'd never experienced before. It was primitive sex—hot, urgent—and she wanted to ride this maelstrom with him.

If they worked off enough frustration they'd be able to talk calmly and she'd be forgiven sooner. Besides, there was nothing wrong with channeling their anger into something that afforded them a great deal of pleasure…

Kade's fingers working the zipper of her jeans pulled her back into pleasure. He pushed her pants and her thong down to her ankles. Brodie stepped out of her backless wedges and kicked her feet free as Kade placed one hand behind her butt and lifted her up and into him. His tongue invaded her mouth again and she knew this would be hot and fast and crazy.

Bring it on!

Matching his urgency, she pulled his shirt up his back and over his head, forcing him to let her go so she could pull it off his arms. She ran her hands down his torso—she'd missed his body, missed *him*, more than she should. Far more than was healthy.

She hated that but she loved this. Loved his hot, masculine, hair-roughened skin. She placed her mouth on his chest to taste him as her hands dropped to his shorts, pulling his belt open with unsteady hands. She needed to feel him in her grasp, needed to taste him on her tongue, to fill her, to complete her.

She needed him.

She both loved and hated the need he stirred inside her.

Kade pushed her hands aside and quickly stripped. She reached down to touch him but he grabbed her wrists to stop her. He encircled them with one hand; easily restraining her while his other hand gripped her jaw and tipped her face up so her eyes collided with his.

Anger and desire were both still there. "We probably shouldn't do this."

"I know." Brodie licked her lips. "But I want to anyway."

"You sure?" Kade demanded, his voice rough. "Because it's not going to be pretty. I'm going to ride you, hard."

Brodie lifted her chin. "I can take everything you hand out, Webb. I'm not a hothouse flower."

The fingers on her jaw loosened and his touch turned tender. "Dammit, Brodie." He rested his forehead against hers.

It was her turn to touch his jaw, to allow her fingers to walk over his face. "You won't hurt me and I need you. I need you so damn much."

Those amazing eyes hardened, just a fraction. There was hurt beneath the anger and she was sorry for it. "You could've fooled me."

Brodie gave him what she could. "Right now, I need you as much as you need me. Give me that, Kade. The rest we can fight about later."

"And we will fight."

"I know." But that was for later so Brodie stood up on her tiptoes to align her mouth with his.

"How are we going to do this?" she whispered against his lips. "Where are we going to do this? Bedroom? Couch?"

Kade's eyes darted around the room. "Too far. Too civilized."

He spun her around and placed her hands on the hall table. Standing behind her, he put his palm on her stomach and pulled up her butt. Brodie swallowed, ferociously excited. So this was...new.

Kade's hand stroked her spine and her lower back, kneaded her butt before sliding between her cheeks to find the damp, moisture between her legs. She heard him sigh and then he was sliding inside her, the position filling her more deeply than he ever had before.

She felt exposed and dominated, but thrilled to her core, which he happened to be touching. His arms encompassed her, crisscrossing her from chest to thigh, and she felt protected and enveloped as her climax built. He was so deep inside he hardly needed to move and his thrusts turned gentle. Bright white lights sparked in her head as the warm, rushing wave pummeled her.

She screamed; he groaned. He pumped against her, once, twice, and then he exploded inside her, his arms tightening as a shudder ran through his body. Slowly coming back to herself, Brodie realized her fingernails were digging into Kade's forearms. The only thing keeping her from doing a face-plant on the floor was Kade's python-like grip. She sucked in a shallow breath and felt his lips on her neck. She was still half-dressed, her bra and shirt still on.

Whoa, Nelly.

Kade's arms loosened and he pulled her upright, sliding out as he did so. He dropped one arm but kept the other around her waist, anchoring her to his side. Brodie stared at the oil painting above the hall table and wondered if she could ever look at it again without remembering the hot sex they'd had beneath it.

"You okay?" Kade asked, his voice low, rough.

Brodie cleared her throat and nodded. "Yeah."

"I didn't hurt you?"

Brodie looked down at his arms and saw the deep

grooves her nails had left in his skin. She traced her fingertip over the marks. "I should be asking you that."

"I'm good." Kade's arm tightened once and his hands flexed on her hips before he let her go. He picked up her jeans and handed them to her. "Go on up. I'll get clean downstairs."

Normally they'd shower together after sex and frequently showering would lead to round two. Brodie sighed. Guess that wasn't going to happen today.

He was still mad. Well, he'd warned her. Brodie nodded and walked toward the stairs, embarrassed he would watch her bare butt the whole way.

But when she turned around at the top of the stairs he'd disappeared to the lower level and his solitary shower.

Wishing she could run away again, Brodie headed into his bedroom and the en suite bathroom. She wouldn't get away with running again.

Brodie found Kade on the balcony, dressed in a faded pair of jeans and a pale blue T-shirt. He sat close to the edge, his bare feet resting on the railings, a beer in his hand. Brodie, dressed in the clothes she'd arrived in, saw there was a diet cola and a glass on the table so she sat down and perched on the cushion.

Kade poured her cola into the ice-filled glass and handed her the cold drink. He sat back and linked his hands behind his head looking like the urban, relaxed businessman he was. Except she also saw the tension in his jaw, the banked anger in his glittering eyes.

"You missed your doctor's appointment and the first ultrasound."

"I called and rescheduled."

"Thanks for letting me know," Kade said, his tone bitter.

Brodie frowned. She'd briefly mentioned the appointment to him and he'd never indicated his intention to go with her. "I didn't know you were planning to go with me."

Kade cut her a look. "Of course I was, Brodie."

Wow…okay. "I thought you'd only take an interest in the baby once it was born."

"I. Take. An. Interest. In. You." Kade spat out the words.

"Oh."

After a couple of minutes, Kade broke the silence. "I was worried about you. I thought something had happened to you, to our baby. I couldn't find you. I didn't know where to start looking."

Brodie closed her eyes at the note of desolation in his voice, the hurt he was trying so hard to hide. Brodie turned her head and looked at his hard profile, the way the evening breeze picked up his hair and blew it over his forehead.

"My dad did that once."

Oh, God, no.

"Did what?" she asked, not really wanting to

know the answer because she knew it would make her feel ten times worse than she already did.

"Disappeared. I was about ten and I came home from school and he wasn't around. By eight that night I was worried, by midnight I was terrified. Three days later I was out of food and out of my mind with worry. Ten years old and I had cramps in my stomach from hunger. The morning of the fourth day I decided to skip school and go to the police. I was leaving the house when he pulled into the driveway, looking like he'd rather be anywhere rather than back in whatever town that was, with me."

Brodie gripped the arms of her chair and closed her eyes, silently cursing Kade's waste-of-space parent. She heard Kade stand up and felt the brief kiss on the top of her head. "I was terrified then but that had nothing on what I felt this past week." Kade's voice sounded like it had been roughened with sandpaper. "Everything is up in the air with us and I get that. I don't want to take over your life or control it or you. But if—when—you go, keep in contact, okay?"

Brodie nodded once, sharply, and forced the words past the tears in her throat. "I don't know what you want from me, Kade."

Kade walked around the chair and stood between her and the railing, the dim lights on the balcony casting shadows over his taut face. "I have no idea, either. I'm as confused about where to go, what to do as you are. But the one thing I do know for sure is that running away doesn't help. My father ran from town to town, from creditor to creditor, nothing ever changed. Because wherever you go, there you are."

Kade's fingers raked through his hair. "But maybe you could talk to me before you run. And I need you to come to grips with having me in your life. Because, even if we aren't going to be together, I am still going to be part of your life because—" he pointed to her midsection "—that is my kid, as well. We're in this together. So, on some level, I need you to trust me, to believe I won't let you down."

But he would. Everyone did.

Before she could respond, he continued, "But, Brodie, you only get this one chance. You run again and that's it. That's you telling me you don't want me in your life, in any capacity."

Brodie bit her bottom lip. "And the baby?"

"I will not abandon my child." Kade rubbed the back of his neck. "Lawyers, supervised visits until the baby is old enough and formal arrangements for custody. We'll be handing over the baby in parking lots. We'll be apart and separate, co-parenting but not communicating."

God, that sounded…awful. Dismal. Depressing.

"Don't do that to us, Brodie. Don't make it like that," Kade said, his voice soft. "I'm not asking for anything other than for you to let me in. To share something of yourself, to trust a little, or even a lot."

Kade's hand drifted over her hair and he bent down to kiss her temple. "I'm going to bed. Feel free to join me. Let me know if you decide to leave."

Brodie nodded.

"And Brodie?"

"Yes?"

"Don't ever ignore my calls again, okay?"

Brodie tied the laces on her running shoes, brimming with energy. Her morning sickness was all but gone and she felt energized and healthy and ready to resume exercising. She wasn't going to hurtle around Stanley Park like she normally did but she'd get her heart rate up and her blood flowing. Surely that had to be good for the baby?

Brodie left her apartment and skipped down the stairs, thinking she still missed her early-morning runs with Kade. So much had changed since they'd first met. She was carrying Kade's baby, they were having hot sex, sometimes at his apartment and, like last night, sometimes at hers. After their fight last week, she was doing her best to be more open, to communicate better.

She loved spending time with him and she couldn't help wondering whether he felt the same, if he missed her at all when she wasn't around? Oh, she knew he liked her, he adored making love with her, but was that the sum total of his feelings? Was he feeling more, wanting more?

Because, dammit, *she* was starting to want more.

Brodie nibbled the inside of her lip. She'd promised herself she wouldn't do this again, with any man, but she was sliding further and further down this slippery slope that might be love. With every smile, every conversation with Kade, she felt another one of her walls dissolving. Soon she'd be stripped bare and at the mercy of the vagaries of life and love. It would hurt.

And how would she ever know if Kade truly loved her and not the idea of her as the mother of his child? What if they became too swept up in playing the happy family and when the novelty wore off he decided this wasn't what he'd signed up for and bolted? How would she cope then?

No, teetering on the edge of love or not, she couldn't risk relying on him and being let down. People always thought they wanted one thing and then it turned out they wanted another. Sure, everyone had a right to change their minds, but she'd prefer it wasn't her heart Kade practiced on.

She'd rather be his friend and his part-time lover for as long as that lasted. When it ended, she'd still be his friend. And he'd be hers. She could do that…

Possibly.

Brodie pulled open the front door, ran down the pathway and bumped smack into a bunch of men standing on the curb. Cameras flashed and she lifted a hand to shield her eyes. What the hell?

"How long have you being seeing Kade?"

"When are you due?"

"Is it a boy or a girl?

"When did you and Kade hook up? Before you matched him?"

"Are you getting married?"

She didn't need to be a rocket scientist to realize the press knew Kade was the father of her baby and she wasn't going for a run this morning.

"You owe us a statement, Ms. Stewart."

"She owes you nothing, Johnson." Kade's deep voice broke through the shouting. Brodie looked up and there he was, holding out a hand. His car was idling behind the reporters and it represented safety and quiet, both of which she needed right now. Brodie grabbed his hand and allowed him to pull her through the throng of reporters.

"Aw, come on, Kade. We need something."

"I can give you a swift kick if that would help." Kade opened the passenger door for Brodie and she slipped inside. Kade shut her door but she could still hear the questions, the demands. Then the crowd quieted and Brodie looked out the window to see that Kade, his back to her and blocking the cameras, had quieted the crowd. "You guys can take potshots at me, ask me anything, but Brodie is off-limits."

"How long have you been together?"

"Are you getting married? Are you living together?"

"Was her matchmaking you just a publicity stunt? Did you lead those women on?"

"Has Myra accepted your offer to buy the franchise? We hear that the rookie is going to sue you personally."

Kade didn't say another word but walked around

the car to the driver's seat. He opened his door and dropped inside. He slammed the door shut but rolled down his window.

"You said we can ask you anything. Not fair, Webb!"

Kade grinned. "I said you can ask me anything, I never said I would answer." Kade started the car, floored the accelerator and drove off. Brodie turned around in her seat to look at the agitated crowd behind them.

"They do not look happy."

"Screw them." Kade veered the car around the corner.

Brodie grabbed her seat belt and pulled it over her chest, clicking it into place. She looked at the creeping speedometer and bit her lip, tasting fear in the back of her throat. "Slow down, please?"

Kade sent her a quick look, then immediately slowed down and placed his hand on her knee. "Sorry. You okay?"

"Fine," Brodie replied, looking at his annoyed profile. "So, how did they find out? Did Wren do a press release?"

"No." Kade shook his head. "We were trying to delay it as long as possible, to put some distance between you becoming pregnant and arranging those stupid dates for me."

"So how did they find out?"

"Someone recognized us when we went to see the ob-gyn."

Brodie twisted her lips. "Anyone in the waiting room could've leaked the story, could've taken a photograph of us."

"And they did. They sold the story to the tabloids and the paper that broke the news has had a photographer following us for at least two weeks. We're a double-page spread," Kade told her, driving in the direction of his apartment.

"Dammit." Brodie sighed. "Guess I am now, officially, one of Webb's Women."

"You are Webb's only woman." He glanced down at her stomach. "Unless there's a girl in there, then you'll have to share the spotlight."

He was using a jokey, upbeat tone and she didn't know whether he was being serious or not. He placed his free hand on her tummy but kept his eyes on the road. "Twenty-six weeks, Brodes, and we'll know."

Kade glided to a smooth stop in front of a traffic light and turned his head to look at her.

"God, the press will eat you up and spit you out."

"I am tougher than I look, Webb." The light turned green and Kade accelerated away.

"Just keep saying 'no comment.' Maybe you should move in with me—my place is a lot more secure than yours."

That wasn't going to happen. Brodie noticed Kade's eyes were dark with worry and his jaw was rock-hard with tension. She knew he cared for her, that he loved making love with her, but even after her trip to California and their fight, she hadn't been sure of how much until this moment. He was genuinely worried for her. Did that mean he loved her?

Stop jumping to conclusions. You're getting way ahead of yourself.

If she moved into the loft, then there was no way she'd be able to keep any emotional distance from him. Whenever they were together she found herself leaning into his shoulder, almost grabbing his hand, and she spent far too much time staring at his mouth.

"Nothing is going to happen to me. I'm healthy, the baby is healthy. And I can deal with the press."

Kade tapped his finger against his steering wheel. "Tell me again in two weeks when they are still shouting questions at you every time you step outside," he muttered.

"I'll be fine." Really, how bad could it be?

Eleven

"I feel like I've answered a million questions about me, what about you?"

Brodie clicked Save on her tablet and watched her database update before her eyes. She recognized the flirtation in the man's voice, the barely disguised interest. She glanced down at her bare ring finger and wished she was wearing her fake engagement ring. It had been a brilliant way to deflect unwanted male attention.

Thanks to the media that wasn't going to work anymore.

Ross Kimball was new to Vancouver, a marine biologist, and he knew no one in the city. During her hour-long interview she'd ascertained he was wealthy, judging by his nice suit, expensive watch and designer shoes. He'd only been in the city a month, he knew nothing about ice hockey, which was brilliant since she was tired of being gossip-column fodder and if she heard the words *Kade's baby-mama* bandied about again she'd stab someone with a fork.

For this moment in time she was Brodie again, matchmaker and businesswoman, and not the woman Kade impregnated. Win.

"As soon as I receive your background report and after I receive your first payment, I'll start the process."

Ross smiled. "Great. Would you like another cup of tea? Juice? Coffee?"

Brodie started to refuse but then she saw loneliness flicker in his eyes. What would it hurt to spend ten minutes talking to this guy? And it would be refreshing to talk to someone who did not want to discuss her and Kade and the baby she was expecting. Instead of refusing she nodded and leaned back in her chair. "Okay. I'll have an orange juice."

They spoke of the weather and the city and Ross's impressions of her hometown. "So, how did you become a matchmaker?" Ross asked.

Brodie gave him the standard spiel and when she was finished, added softly, "I hope I find you someone you can connect with."

"Are you…connected with anyone?"

She'd opened the door to these questions so she'd give him a little leeway. "It's complicated."

"It usually is."

"I'm seeing a guy. We're friends. Good friends."

"You're not in love with him?"

How could she answer when she wasn't sure what the answer was? How could she be in love with Kade when what they had was so different from what she had before? Jay had been sunshine and light, easy-going and happy-go-lucky. Kade was powerful, frequently sarcastic and reticent. The two men were galaxies apart. How could she possibly love such wildly differing men?

Was it love or was it just lust?

"What are you thinking about?" Ross asked.

"The difference between love and lust," Brodie replied.

"Tell me."

"Love is an intense affection for each other. It takes times to grow." Like fifteen years. "Lust is based on physical attraction." Lust was wanting to jump Kade every time he walked into the room. "It can transform into love over time. Love is about how interconnected two people are."

She and Kade were having a baby together. How much more interconnected could they be? He knew about Jay and her parents. Her great-aunt regularly called his cell for a chat. His friends had become hers, she was far more comfortable in his loft than she was in her own apartment and he'd taken her car to be serviced. She picked up his laundry.

They were interconnected.

Maybe she loved him. But that thought made her feel intensely guilty because this bubbling mess of feelings she had for Kade was deeper and darker and harder and crazier than she'd ever felt for Jay. She had survived his death. She knew without qualification she could not live in a world that did not have Kade in it.

God, this was crazy! What had happened to her? Why was she doing this? She knew what it felt like to love and lose, and what if she allowed herself to delve into this emotion and all he wanted to be was her friend with brilliant benefits? What if he, tomorrow or the next day or the year after that, met the love of his life and decided to move on from her, from them? How would she stand it? How would she cope seeing him and talking to him and co-parenting with him while knowing he left her to sleep in another woman's bed? That he was holding another woman, loving her, laughing with her?

Brodie was such a fool. This had to stop. She had to pull herself back from the brink, to keep control. Yes, withdrawing from Kade would hurt but it would be nothing compared to what could happen down the line.

She could do this; she had to do this.

"Wow. That was one hell of a trip you took," Ross said, his expression speculative.

"Sorry." Brodie picked up her juice and took a long swallow. "What were we talking about?"

"Your fellow and whether you were in love with him."

"I don't believe in love." The words flew out of Brodie's mouth. Seeing his startled expression, she wished she could take them back. But then, suddenly, it was more important someone listen to what she was *saying*. Because if she could convince him, then maybe she could convince herself.

"At least not for me. I believe in sex. I believe in friendships, in being independent, in standing on my own two feet. I believe in my career, in forging my own path, in keeping an emotional distance."

"He's not the one?"

Brodie made herself meet his eyes, trying to talk herself off the ledge. "I'm having his baby and, admittedly, he's stuck around but I don't expect he'll stay for much longer. Having a baby is a novelty, a whim, and he'll lose interest. He has a low boredom threshold."

Oh, God, nothing was further from the truth, and verbalizing those lies didn't change how she felt about him. They just made her feel nasty and bitchy and guilty, dammit!

Under the table she patted her tummy and silently spoke to her child. "Ignore that, kiddo, your dad is not like that. In fact, the problem is that he is utterly wonderful. I just don't know how to handle him."

* * *

Kade stood in front of the six-by-eight-foot oil painting dominating one wall of the gallery and reluctantly admitted his father was a ridiculously talented artist.

He recognized the scene—it was the view from the rickety back porch of a cabin in Pleasant, a town north of Whitehorse. He hadn't seen the snow-covered mountains, the icy beauty of the scene, he just remembered his skates had been too small and he'd had holes in his parka. And the cupboards had held little more than bread and cereal. His father had just spent the last of his money on more oil paints, a canvas and brushes.

Kade looked at the familiar signature in the bottom corner and waited for the flood of resentment and the bite of pain that usually accompanied it. When neither arrived, he took a step back and cocked his head, wondering what had changed. His father was his father and his childhood hadn't been a barrel of laughs, but it was, thank God, long over. Being his father's son had taught him resilience, how to be tough, that nothing came to people who didn't work their asses off. James's success was proof of that. He'd been consumed by his art and had thrown everything he had into it and, judging by the fact that this painting was on sale for seventy-five thousand dollars, sacrificing a relationship with his son had been worth it.

Kade blew out his breath, finding it strange not to

feel bitter. He really didn't, not anymore. His father was his father, selfish and obsessive. Nothing was important to his father but his art. That there was no hint of the child who explored the country with him in any of the paintings exhibited was a pretty big clue he wouldn't care that he was about to become a grandfather.

Art was all that mattered.

Kade had felt like that about his career until Brodie dropped back into his life. Suddenly he had to—wanted to—think about someone else. He couldn't work fourteen- or sixteen-hour days anymore. He needed to find a balance between work and home, especially when the baby arrived. Besides, he didn't want to spend so much time at work. He enjoyed Brodie's company and he wanted to spend time with his child. He would not be his father's son.

Kade turned away from the painting, finally at peace with the fact that he would never have a relationship with James. He'd lost his father a long time ago, if he'd ever really had him. Kade could finally put these particular demons to rest.

With a considerably lighter heart Kade left the gallery. As he stepped onto the sidewalk, he felt his cell vibrate. He read the incoming message from Wren and clicked on the link she provided.

A reporter had gotten Brodie to open up—through subterfuge, but still. Worse, he'd gotten her to talk about how she was feeling, something Kade had difficulty doing. Strange that it should hurt so much. She could talk to strangers but not to him?

And then there was what she'd said to the blogger, scumbag that he was. Her words had Kade feeling like a clawed hand was ripping his heart apart. She didn't believe in love, didn't want it in her life and didn't believe Kade could provide it.

Despite everything they'd gone through, she still thought he was playing games, that he would bail. He might no longer think he was his father's son but Brodie certainly did, judging by the fact that she'd publicly stated she was expecting him to leave.

Man, that hurt. Even more painful than the hunger, the fear, the uncertainty he'd experienced as a kid. To have the woman in his life thinking so little of him…it felt as if she'd used his heart as a hockey puck.

Why? Kade stared down at his screen, unable to get his feet to move. Why did he care so damn much?

Because he loved her.

Crap, dammit, hell.

Because, like he'd always been with his father, Kade was desperate for her to love him. Because, again like his father had been, Brodie was Kade's world. And, like James, Kade wasn't hers.

How the hell had he let this happen?

Kade started to walk. He needed to move or else he would scream. He was in love with her, she didn't love him. What did he do now? He could walk away, break it off. In a couple of months he could sic his lawyers on her, demanding custody rights, and they could communicate that way. He didn't have to talk to her again if he didn't want to.

He didn't want to; he felt too raw.

Or he could go to her, give her a chance to explain. See if there was anything they could salvage out of this train wreck of a relationship. No, not a relationship; Brodie didn't believe in those… He should just let the lawyers deal with it, with her, but his feet didn't agree. They just kept walking in the direction of Brodie's office.

They might, if he was really lucky, let him walk right on past her building.

It was after eight in the evening and Brodie was exhausted. She couldn't wait to go home, maybe sink into the spa bath, preferably naked, with Kade. Pushing her chair back from her desk, she stood up and winced when the button of her black pants pushed into her stomach. She was going to have to buy some bigger clothes. Her tummy was growing at an alarming rate and, unfortunately, she suspected her bottom was following the trend.

Maybe Kade could show her some exercises she could safely do to keep her butt from spreading. Her tummy was on its own.

Brodie opened her lower drawer to pull out her bag and sighed when her computer signaled the arrival of a new email. She'd never been able to ignore a ringing phone or a new message so she clicked the mouse.

What?

It took a moment for her to make sense of the words on the screen. It was from the company she and Colin used to run background reports. It was fairly important their clients were who they said they were. That they weren't broke, had a criminal record…

Because she was swamped with clients this week, she'd done the interview with Kimball before she received the background checks, something she didn't like to do. If she had waited, she would've known Ross Kimball was not who he said he was. He wasn't living at the address he stated; there were no marine biologists working in the area, or in the country, under that name and his contact numbers were bogus.

Brodie pulled out her chair and sat down. She'd been played and played well. Who was Kimball and why had he used such an elaborate ruse to meet her?

It didn't take her long to come up with an answer.

Kade. And her relationship with him.

Since the world found out she was carrying Kade's baby—*a new generation of Mavericks!*—she'd been bombarded with requests for interviews and she'd refused every offer. Her standard response was a consistent and, she guessed, infuriating "no comment."

As Kade had said, the press had gone looking for a story and Ross had sneaked in via the back door. He'd played the role well, she thought. She hadn't once suspected he wasn't who he said he was.

So, who did he work for and what had he penned? And how could she find out, preferably before Wren and Kade did?

What had she told the man? They'd discussed the city and how lonely it could be, he'd flirted with her and she'd shut him down…

Shut him down by telling him she didn't believe in love…

"'Brodie Stewart is a walking contradiction, someone who earns a very healthy living matching people in that eternal quest for true love while discounting the notion for herself.'"

Brodie jerked her head up and winced when she saw Kade standing in the doorway to her office, reading from his phone. Well, guess she didn't have to go looking for the article. Kade—via the annoyingly efficient Wren, she presumed—had accessed it on his smartphone. And, judging by his furious expression, he was less than thrilled by its contents.

Brodie leaned her head against the back of her chair. "Who is he?"

"Ross Bennett. A blogger with an enormous following. Quite well-known for his ability to twist the truth," Kade replied, looking back down at the screen. Then he started to read, his tone flat and terrifyingly devoid of all emotion.

> "In an interview with Ms. Stewart, she candidly admitted she didn't believe in love. 'I believe in sex. I believe in being independent, of

standing on my own two feet. I believe in my career, in forging my own path, in keeping an emotional distance.'

"She doesn't seem to have much faith in Kade Webb, either. Webb, according to Ms. Stewart, won't stick around for the long haul. To Kade, having a baby is a novelty and she expects him to lose interest."

Brodie gripped the arms of her chair. Oh, this was bad. This was very bad.

"Luckily for the Mavericks, Bennett is regarded as a trash-talking, sensation-seeking journalist. He is best to be ignored. Wren thought he was sucking the story out of thin air, but I heard your voice in those words. What happened?"

"He posed as a client and he fooled me," Brodie reluctantly admitted.

Kade leaned a shoulder into the wall, his face a blank mask. His eyes were flat and emotionless and his mouth was a hard line. Kade was, she knew, incandescently angry. Maybe this was the final straw; she'd pushed him away so many times…maybe this time she'd pushed him too far. She'd tested his commitment to sticking by her and their child and he'd passed every test. But this was no longer a game, she realized; she'd pushed too hard and too far.

She didn't need him to verbalize his intentions; he was done. The moment she'd both dreaded and welcomed was here and the pain would follow. She would deal with it and then she would go back to her safe, emotion-free life.

The life she wanted, she reminded herself. The life she felt comfortable in. The lonely, color-free, safe, boring life.

"Did I ever give you reason to think I would fade away?"

"No."

"That I was playing at being a father?"

Brodie shook her head.

"I read that blog while standing outside the gallery exhibiting my father's latest work. It struck me you could've been describing my father—that's the way he was, the way he acted."

God, she hadn't thought of that. Hadn't meant him to think that. He was *nothing* like the man who sired him. "I'm sorry."

"Being sorry doesn't help, neither does how I feel about you." Kade shook his head. "I can't keep doing this, Brodie. I can't fight your fear anymore, you've got to do that yourself. I told you I'll be here for you but you don't want to believe it and I can't force you to."

Kade shoved a hand into his hair. "For you to think that, verbalize it, means you either believe it or you want to believe it. It doesn't matter which. Either way it tells me you are intolerant of intimacy and you deliberately cut yourself off. And this—" Kade showed her the screen "—this is you running. I'm not going to be the sap who runs after you, begging you to give me another chance. I did that with my father, I will not do it again. I've given you enough chances. I'm worth more than that and, frankly, so are you."

Brodie felt the kick in her stomach, in her heart, in her head. "Okay."

"Okay? That's it? That's all you have to say?"

She wouldn't throw herself at his knees and beg him not to leave her. It was better this way; it had to be. "What do you want to do about the baby?"

"The baby? God!" Kade looked like he wanted to put his fist through a wall. "Right now I'm so damn mad at you I can't think! Do you not understand you are throwing away something pretty amazing to hide behind those walls you've built up? I'm scared, too, Brodie. Raising kids, being together, is meant to be scary!"

"There are no guarantees, Kade."

"Of course there aren't! You just take what happiness you can and run with it. You just feel damn grateful for it." Kade rubbed his hands over his face. "I'm talking to a freaking brick wall. Have fun hiding out, Brodie. As I said, I'm done."

Brodie nodded once and bit her bottom lip, everything in her trying to keep the tears at bay. "Okay."

"Okay? That's all you have? For God's sake..." Kade slapped his hand against the door frame as he whipped around. "Talking to a friggin' wall."

Brodie waited until she heard the door to the outer office slam closed before she finally allowed herself to cry. Hunched over and hurting, she watched from a place far away as tears ran off her face and dropped to the carpet below.

Yeah, the pain was here, accompanied by desolation and despair. It was okay, she'd been here before and she'd handled it.

She could do it again.

But right now she just wanted to cry, for herself, for her child, for the butterflies in her stomach that were dying a slow and excruciating death.

Kade was convinced he held the record for the fastest heartbreak in the history of the world. Within the space of the afternoon he'd realized he loved Brodie and that nothing would ever come of it. His mind wanted to stop loving her but he knew his heart always would.

Kade loosened his tight grip on the stem of his wineglass and stared at False Creek, for the first time not seeing the beauty below him. It had been twilight when he returned home from work tonight, three weeks since he'd walked out of Brodie's office and her life. And while he could remember the exact date and time his life turned dark, he had no idea what time it was now.

Brodie had done what he'd expected, maintained radio silence. They hadn't spoken, messaged, emailed or texted each other and he felt adrift. Before Brodie hurtled her way into his life he'd felt content with his lot, generally happy. He hadn't wanted a relationship and had been content to have an affair here, a one-night stand there. No promises, no hassle.

Brodie had been nothing but a hassle and an all-around pain in his ass, but when she wasn't annoying him, she brought light and laughter to his life. Kade placed his forearm over his eyes and cursed his burning eyes.

He finally loved someone with everything he had and she wanted jack from him. Life was laughing at him.

He wanted to go to Brodie, wanted to beg her to allow him to be part of her life, but he knew that was a road heading straight to a deeper level of hell. He'd be seeing her again in five months or so anyway, and maybe by then he would've stopped thinking about what they could've had.

Growing up with his father had taught Kade that chasing rainbows led to disappointment. You couldn't force someone to love you. Love wasn't something to be demanded; it either was or it…wasn't.

He loved Brodie and while he suspected she could love him, she didn't. She wouldn't allow herself to love him and he wasn't going to beg. He wanted everything and he wouldn't settle for anything less. He couldn't; the resentment would kill him and, worse, it would kill his love for her.

So he'd love her from a distance for the rest of his life. That was the way it had to be so the sooner he got used to feeling like crap, the better.

Kade sat up, rested his forearms on his thighs

and dangled the glass between his knees. He could wallow or he could distract himself. He could call Quinn and they could go clubbing. He could go to Mac and Rory's for dinner. He could do some work or a gym session.

What he wasn't going to do was to sit on this couch in the dark and feel sorry for himself. Yet it was another fifteen minutes before he got up and another ten before he crossed the room to flick on some lights.

He just needed time, he told himself. A millennium or two might be long enough to get over her.

Twelve

The summer holidays were almost over and the vast beaches on the west side of Vancouver Island had been, for all intents and purposes, returned to the birds and the crabs that were the year-round residents of the island. Soon the leaves would start to turn, winter would drop the temperature and the storms would roll in.

But for now, Brodie and Poppy walked the empty beach, bare feet digging into the sand, watching the rolling waves kiss the shore. The stiff breeze pushed Brodie's thin hoodie against her round tummy and kicked sand up against her bright blue yoga pants. She loved this place, Brodie realized. Away from

Vancouver, away from the city, she could breathe and think.

"When are you going to stop punishing yourself for living?" Poppy asked as she took Brodie's arm.

Brodie pushed a hunk of hair out of her eyes and squinted at Poppy. "I'm not punishing myself."

"Really? Well, the way I see it there is a man on the mainland who wants to be part of your life, who wants to raise this baby with you, but you are determined to take the hard road and do it all by your little lonesome. Is that not punishing yourself?"

"That's me protecting myself," Brodie retorted.

"From what? Pain?" Poppy asked. "From loneliness?"

Brodie stared out to sea and focused her attention on a ship on the horizon and ignored Poppy's probing questions. She didn't want to think about Kade, though there was little else she thought about these days. She definitely didn't want to talk about him.

But Poppy wasn't intimidated by Brodie's scowling face or her frown. "News flash, you are so damn lonely you don't know what to do with yourself."

"Pops, please."

Poppy dropped her arm and they stood side by side, looking out to sea. Poppy released a long breath. "Do you see that ship?"

She'd only been staring at it for the past half hour. Brodie nodded, glad Poppy had dropped the subject of Kade. "It's a container ship, probably headed for Japan."

Poppy nodded, her expression contemplative. "There's a saying about ships and leaving the harbor...do you know it?"

Brodie shook her head.

"It goes something like this—'a ship in the harbor is safe, but that's not what ships are built for.'"

Brodie wrinkled her nose. How silly she'd been to think Poppy had dropped the subject; Poppy only stopped when she'd brought you around to her way of thinking.

"Ships aren't built for safety but neither are humans. We should take risks. We *have* to take risks. You and Kade? Well, that's a risk worth taking."

"I'm scared. Of loving him too much, scared it won't last forever. Scared he thinks he loves me but only loves me because of this baby. So scared he might—"

"Die?" Poppy interrupted. "What if you die? What if a freak tsunami washes you off the beach right now? What then? What if you die giving birth? What then?"

"That would suck," Brodie admitted.

"It really would. But would you want Kade to be alone for the rest of his life, to—metaphorically speaking—wear black widower's weeds, too scared to love again, laugh again? To live again?"

Dammit. She knew where Poppy was going with this but she couldn't find anything to say to get out of this quandary. All she could think of was that it was easier for Poppy to say it than for Brodie to do it.

"Well?" Poppy demanded.

"But—"

"There are no buts. Jay would hate to see you like this. Your parents would be so disappointed in you." Poppy grabbed Brodie's chin and forced her to meet faded blue eyes. Poppy's body might be old but her eyes were alive and fierce and determined.

"Do you love him?"

Brodie couldn't lie, wouldn't lie. "Yes."

"These are your choices and you need to think them through. You can wallow and live a miserable half life until you die. You can keep punishing yourself, keep disappointing yourself because you don't have the balls to choose differently."

"God, Poppy."

Poppy ignored Brodie's desperate laugh. "Or you can take your butt back to the city, throw yourself at his feet and apologize for being an ass. Find out if he loves you, if this is a forever thing. Face your fears."

"That's a hard decision to make, even harder to do," Brodie protested.

"Do it anyway," Poppy suggested. "Be brave enough to be happy, Brodie. Don't let your fear win. You are stronger than that, more courageous than you think. Just do it, my darling. Reach out and grab the future you've always wanted."

"But what if I'm too late?" Brodie asked, unsure why she was asking this question because she wasn't going to go to Kade, wasn't going to ask for another chance. That was crazy talk…wasn't it?

Poppy's sweet smile held more than a trace of satisfaction. And triumph. "What if you're not?" She placed a wrinkled hand on Brodie's face. "Don't make me get tough with you, Brodie."

"This isn't you being tough?" Brodie demanded with a sarcastic laugh.

"Honey, I haven't even warmed up yet. I can go on for hours," Poppy stated prosaically. "You might as well just give in now and save us both the time and energy."

Brodie put her arms around Poppy's waist and rested her head on her great-aunt's shoulder. "Well, when you put it like that..."

Brodie used her shaking index finger to key in the code that would take her straight up to Kade's apartment. She hoped he hadn't changed the code. That would be mortifying. She entered the last number and waited for the elevator doors to slide open. When they did she had to force herself to step inside.

She could do this. She had to do this.

If she didn't speak to Kade tonight, she never would. She would talk herself out of being brave. She'd allow herself to backslide, to rationalize why she would be better off alone.

Talk the truth, even if your voice shakes.

Poppy's words stuck with Brodie and she repeated them to herself as the elevator took her higher, and closer, to the love of her life.

And he was that. Jay, dear Jay, had been marvelous, but her feelings for Kade were deeper, harder and stronger. Maybe that's why she'd been fighting this so hard. Loving Kade wouldn't be easy but he'd be worth it.

She had to tell him, had to see if he felt the same.

As the elevator stopped at the top floor she touched her stomach in that age-old protective gesture women had been using through the centuries.

Wish me luck, baby. Here's hoping we get to be a family.

Brodie stepped into the dark loft, the lights from downtown Vancouver dancing in the floor-to-ceiling windows. The apartment was ridiculously quiet and she bit her lip, feeling like an idiot. She hadn't considered the notion that Kade might not be here. He could be anywhere—with his friends, out of town, on a date. The only thing worse than Kade coming home with a date would be finding Kade upstairs in bed with another woman. With the doors closed, she wouldn't be able to hear a thing.

It had only been three weeks. He wouldn't have moved on so soon, would he? Then again, she'd kept pushing him away, telling him that what they had was only sex. Maybe he was upstairs, doing all those fabulous things he did to her…

Brodie threw her bag onto the couch and stormed toward the staircase. If she'd been bawling her eyes out while he slept his way through the pack of puck bunnies, Brodie might be forced to do something drastic.

What, she wasn't sure, but it would hurt. A lot.

Brodie flung open the door to his bedroom and hurtled over the threshold, stopping when she realized his enormous bed was neatly made and, crucially, empty. Brodie closed her eyes and hauled in a deep breath.

"You're acting like a crazy woman, Stewart," she muttered.

"Can't say that I disagree."

Brodie whirled around and saw Kade standing in the doorway to his en suite bathroom, a towel wrapped around his narrow hips. Man, he was gorgeous. How could she have walked away from that?

He was sexy and hot but he was also a good man. Someone who was loyal and kind and considerate and…hers.

"What are you doing here, Brodie?" Kade asked, his expression forbidding.

"Uh…" Okay, she was being silly but she just had to make sure. "Is there anyone in there with you?"

Kade turned his head to look back into the bathroom. "Busted. Come on out, honey," he called.

Brodie's heart ker-plunked. She placed a hand on her sternum and tried to find something to say.

"God, Brodie, don't be an idiot," Kade snapped. "There's no one here. I was just messing with you."

Brodie scowled. "Don't do that, okay?"

"I think I've got a right," Kade retorted. He pushed his hand through his wet hair. "I can't stand here, almost naked, with you in the room. Why don't you go downstairs and keep walking across the apartment until you hit the elevator. I doubt there's anything you have to say that I want to hear."

"No." Brodie lifted her chin.

"No?"

"No, I'm not going to do that."

Kade shrugged, sent her a sarcastic smile and walked to his closet. Dropping the towel to the floor, Brodie watched him go into the small room, bare-ass naked. Man, he was so messing with her.

"So why are you here? Missing the sex?" Kade asked as he reached for a pair of sweats.

"Yes," Brodie replied, thinking honesty was the best policy. "Of course I am. We are fabulous together and I love making love with you."

Kade pulled on the sweats and turned, gripping the top of the door frame with white fingers. "Is that what you're back for?" He took in her leggings and bohemian shirt. "Fine. But you're a bit overdressed. Strip."

"Stop being a jerk, Kade," Brodie snapped.

"Then again, if it's just sex you're back for, then I am not interested." Kade dropped his arms. He rubbed his hands over his face and when he looked at her again, those beautiful eyes were bleak. And his voice, when he spoke again, sounded desolate. "Just go, Brodie. Please."

She'd done this, Brodie thought, ashamed of herself. She'd hurt him. She'd wounded this powerful, smart man just because she'd been too scared to take a chance. To live. Well, that stopped now, right this minute. She needed to be better than that; her child—their child—and Kade deserved better. But how to tell him? What to say?

Brodie walked past the bed to the open balcony doors and thought about Vancouver Island. Remembering Poppy and their conversation, Brodie pushed her shoulders back and placed her hands behind her, anchoring herself to the door frame.

"When I was about eleven, I was a bridesmaid and I fell in love with the idea of love. I became slightly obsessed with weddings, with the idea of happily-ever-after. Jay was the boy from down the road and even then, I thought he might be the one."

Brodie risked looking at Kade, relieved to see he was interested in what she was saying. His expression was still remote and, to be honest, scarily forbidding, but he hadn't kicked her out. It was progress but she had a long way to go. "I made a scrapbook. What my dress would look like, the color scheme, my bridesmaids' dresses, the whole shebang."

"Is there a point to this?" Kade asked, impatient.

Brodie ignored him. "Strangely, I pretty much nailed what I wanted for a wedding at eleven. When I flipped open the scrapbook shortly before the accident, excited because Jay and I were moving on from being best friends to something more, there was little I wanted changed. But one aspect jumped out at me and it's been bugging me."

"Pray tell."

Still sarcastic, Brodie sighed. "Jay was dark-haired and blue-eyed, short and stocky," Brodie continued. "My eleven-year-old self didn't have him in mind when she was imagining her groom. Jay looked nothing like the tall, blond, sexy man in my scrapbook."

Kade didn't say anything but Brodie noticed his expression had turned from remote to speculative.

"Do you think my younger self knew something I didn't? Even then? Don't you think that's spooky?"

"I don't give a damn about your eleven-year-old self," Kade stated, his tone brisk. "I want to know what you want, right now."

Right, time to jump off this cliff. God, she hoped he was going to catch her. "You." Her voice cracked with emotion. "I just want you. Any way I can get you."

"Explain that," Kade demanded, his eyes locked on hers.

Brodie wished he would come to her, initiate contact. "This has nothing to do with the fact we have such incredible sexual chemistry, or that you're my baby's father. Or that you are hot, which, I have to say, is a bonus…" Brodie smiled but Kade didn't react. He didn't say a damn thing, just continued to stare at her with those hot, demanding eyes.

Oh, crap. He was going to make her say it. She hauled in a breath and gathered her courage. "I love you. I just want to be with you." Brodie bit her bottom lip. "I'm so sorry about what I said, did. I was trying to fall out of love with you. But I need you to know I believe you are nothing like your father, that I know you will be a spectacular dad."

Kade rubbed his jaw and then the back of his neck. "Jesus, Brodie."

"I'm sorry. For everything I said because I was so damn scared." Brodie stared at her red ballet pumps. She turned her head and looked at Kade. He seemed gobsmacked and, she had to admit, not very damn happy at her proclamation. She'd been too late. She'd lost him.

Brodie forced her rubbery legs to walk toward the door. She scooped up her bag as she walked past the bed.

"What do you want from me, Brodie?" Kade intercepted her and placed both his hands on her upper arms.

Brodie shrugged. "Nothing you can't give me, openly and honestly. I just want you in my life, any way I can get you. With or without the baby, I love you. It's taken me a while, but now it's suddenly simple. It's fine that you don't love me. I still want you to be my friend, to co-parent with you, to be our baby's dad."

Kade cupped the side of her face with his big hand and she finally saw the beginning of a smile. "For a bright woman, you can be incredibly dense on occasion."

What did that mean? What was he trying to say?

Kade's thumb drifted over her bottom lip, down her chin. "I can love you. I do love you."

Brodie felt her heart expand, fill with a warm, bright light. Before it could start dancing around her rib cage, she grabbed it in an iron fist. "In what way?"

"In every way that counts. " Kade kissed the corner of her mouth. "And more. A lot more."

She loosened the hold on her heart. "Meaning?"

"Meaning I love you, too. I will always love you. I never expected this to happen to me, not like this. We met again and I feel like I've been riding a hurricane and I've loved every minute. You drive me nuts, you turn me on. I think about you all the damn time." He swallowed some emotion and Brodie blinked back her tears.

"I imagine the family we can have, the fun we'll have," Kade continued, "I dream about the love that will color our lives."

Brodie smiled slowly, her heart dancing. She placed her hands on his pecs and rested her forehead on his chest. "Oh, God, I feel light-headed. I am so relieved." Kade's hand cupped the back of her head. "While I was running away, I realized I'd so rather be scared with you than be without you. I'd rather stand in an electrical storm with you than be safe by myself. You're my it, Kade—the blond, big man my eleven-year-old self recognized so long ago."

"Brodie." Kade's arms tightened around her and easily lifted her so her mouth aligned with his. "Welcome home, baby. Don't run away anymore."

"Thank you for giving me another chance," she murmured against his lips.

"I've missed you." A mischievous smile crossed his face as humor and relief chased the last residue of hurt and disappointment from his eyes. "So does this mean I have to get rid of the girl in the bathroom?"

Brodie tapped on the door to Kade's office and popped her head in. It was the end of the day and her man sat behind his desk, his fingers flying across his keyboard. He looked up and the frown on his face disappeared as his smile reached his eyes. They'd been back together for a month and the butterflies in her stomach were still going mad, occasionally accompanied by a tiny flutter that was all Baby Webb.

"Hey, gorgeous." Kade leaned back in his chair as she closed the door behind her. She walked over to his desk and plopped herself into his lap, lifting her face for a thorough, very sexy kiss. Kade pulled away and placed his hand on her round tummy. "How's my other girl?"

"Your *boy* has started to play ice hockey in my womb," Brodie replied. "We have a doctor's appointment next week."

"I haven't forgotten." Kade looked at his watch. "As much as I love the idea of you surprising me at work, I thought you had a late meeting."

"I did but I canceled." She was about to add she forgot to wear her fake engagement ring but she knew that might prompt Kade to suggest he buy her a real ring. She knew a proposal was coming but she wanted to do something different…

Hence her visit to his office.

Brodie climbed off his lap and sat on the edge of his desk so she could see his face. “So, Wren called me and told me she’s posted the final blog on our endeavor to find your happily-ever-after.”

“You’re my happily-ever-after.” Kade placed a hand on her knee. “I told her to take that nonsense down. It’s silly to have it on the site when everyone knows we are together, a couple, in love and that we are having a baby.”

“Still—” Brodie tapped her finger on the screen of his laptop “—take a look.”

“You’ve seen it?” Kade asked, sitting up.

“I approved it. I hope you do, too.” She licked her lips and watched as he double-clicked the icon on the screen to bring up the Mavericks’ website. He went to the relevant page and started to read. Brodie tucked her shaking hands under her thighs and read along with him.

There was a photo of them in the top right-hand corner with the words *Kade’s future* as a title.

> As a matchmaker, I have matched many couples and it gives me great pleasure to play a small part in helping people find happiness in love. I have, in the process of trying to find Kade’s life partner, found the same happiness

and nobody was more surprised than I was when I realized Kade was mine.

I never thought that love, permanence and commitment would be a part of my future again but I am honored and thrilled to have found it with Kade.

He and our child are my future, my joy, my heart. So, sorry, ladies of Vancouver, but Kade Webb is officially and permanently off the market.

Yours,

Brodie

Brodie found her courage and said the words she'd been practicing for the past week. "So, my mom's engagement ring is very real and I'd like to wear it. Are you game, Webb?"

Brodie watched as Kade slowly turned and sent her his charming, emotional, full-blown smile. He leaned back in his chair and linked his hands across his stomach. "You proposing, Stewart?"

Brodie lifted one shoulder. "It's a suggestion..."

"I like your suggestion," Kade softly answered her.

Warmth coursed through her, relaxing and rejuvenating her at the same time.

Kade gestured to the screen. "Why this, Brodes? It's a pretty public declaration."

That was the point. Brodie attempted to explain. "I know, it'll be the only time I'll ever do or say something about us on social media, but I needed to.

I've lived in the shadows for so long. I've protected myself so well, I wanted to show you exactly how committed I am to you, to us. I wanted you to know I'm still scared but I'm not going to run away." She stared at her shoes. "Maybe it was just me breaking through my cocoon."

Kade stood and tipped up her face. "Thank you." He placed his hands on the desk and dropped a sexy, sweet kiss on her mouth. "I love you so damn much and I can't wait to marry you. Hand the ring over and I'll do the bended-knee thing."

Brodie grinned. "I can't wait to see you on bended knee and I love you back."

Kade smiled against her lips. "First and last time. Now that our future is sorted, let's talk about the important stuff."

"Where we're going to live—your loft—and when we're going to get married? I was thinking the sooner the better."

Kade's eyes glinted. "Actually, I was talking about the *really* important stuff, like how soon I can get you naked—"

The door burst open and they broke off their deep kiss and looked around to see Quinn standing in the doorway.

"Oh, for God's sake, do you two do anything other than grope each other?" he demanded, slapping his hand over his eyes.

"Not really, no." Kade scowled at his friend. "What do you want, jerkoid?"

"Rory's on her way to the hospital, she's in labor. We're going to have our first Maverick baby!"

Kade grabbed his jacket and Brodie's hand. "We're right behind you." At the door he kissed Brodie again and tucked her into his side. "The future looks good, babe."

Brodie sighed and placed a hand on her stomach. "It really does."

And this time, for the first time in far too long, she was convinced of it.

* * * * *

COMING NEXT MONTH FROM

Available September 6, 2016

#2467 THE RANCHER'S ONE-WEEK WIFE

by Kathie DeNosky

Wealthy rancher Blake and city-girl Karly's whirlwind rodeo romance ends with wedding vows—and then reality sets in! But during the delivery of divorce papers, she's stranded at his ranch. Can they turn their one week into forever?

#2468 THE BOSS'S BABY ARRANGEMENT

Billionaires and Babies • by Catherine Mann

A marriage of convenience between an executive single dad and his sexy employee in need of a green card *should* have nothing to do with passion...but their carefully laid plan goes out the window when their hearts become involved!

#2469 EXPECTING HIS SECRET HEIR

Mill Town Millionaires • by Dani Wade

Mission: dig up dirt on Zach Gatlin, so he'll be disqualified from inheriting the fortune he doesn't know exists. Payment: enough money to cover Sadie's critically ill sister's medical bills. Approach: seduction. Complication: her heart...and a baby!

#2470 CLAIMED BY THE COWBOY

Dynasties: The Newports • by Sarah M. Anderson

Cowboy Josh Calhoun is only in Chicago to help a friend, but he unexpectedly gets a second chance with Dr. Lucinda Wilde. He let her go once out of respect for his best friend, but this time he plans to claim her...

#2471 BILLIONAIRE BOSS, M.D.

The Billionaires of Black Castle • by Olivia Gates

As her new boss, billionaire doctor Antonio Balducci plans to use medical researcher Liliana Accardi to destroy those who left him to a hellish fate. But when love unexpectedly overwhelms him, could it overcome his need for vengeance?

#2472 SECOND CHANCE WITH THE CEO

The Serenghetti Brothers • by Anna DePalo

Beautiful Marisa Danieli is the reason former athlete turned CEO Cole Serenghetti missed a major career goal, something he's never forgotten—or forgiven. How unfortunate for her that the sexy tycoon is the one thing standing between her and the promotion she needs...

HARLEQUIN®
A Romance FOR EVERY MOOD™

A marriage of convenience between an executive single dad and his sexy employee in need of a green card should *have nothing to do with passion...but their carefully laid plan goes out the window when their hearts become involved!*

Read on for a sneak peek at THE BOSS'S BABY ARRANGEMENT, by USA TODAY *bestselling author*

Catherine Mann

and part of the bestselling ***BILLIONAIRES AND BABIES*** *series.*

Maureen Burke danced with abandon.

Throwing herself into this pocket of time, matching the steps of this leanly athletic man with charismatic blue eyes and a sexual intensity as potent as his handsome face.

Brains. Brilliance. A body to die for and a loyal love of family.

Xander Lourdes was a good man.

But not her man.

So Maureen allowed herself to dance with the abandon she never would have dared otherwise. Not now. Not after all she'd been through.

She allowed herself to be swept away by the dance, the music and the pulse of the drums pushing through her veins with every heartbeat, faster and faster. Arching timbres of the steel drums urged her to absorb every fiber of this moment.

Too soon, her work visa was due to expire, and officials had thus far denied her requests to extend it. She would have to go

HDEXP0816

home. To face all she'd run from, to leave this amazing place where abandon meant beauty and exuberance. Freedom.

She was free to look now, though, at this man with coal-black hair that spiked with the sea breeze and a hint of sweat. His square jaw was peppered with a five-o'clock shadow, his shoulders broad in his tuxedo, broad enough to carry the weight of the world.

Shivering with warm tingles that had nothing to do with any bonfire or humid night, she could feel the attraction radiating off him the same way it heated in her. She'd sensed the draw before but his grief was so well-known she hadn't wanted to wade into those complicated waters. But with her return to home looming…

Maureen wasn't interested in a relationship, but maybe if she was leaving she could indulge in—

Suddenly his attention was yanked from her. He reached into his tuxedo pocket and pulled out his cell phone and read the text.

Tension pulsed through his jaw, the once-relaxed, half-cocked smile replaced instantly with a serious expression. "It's the nanny. My daughter's running a fever. I have to go."

And without another word, he was gone and she knew she was gone from his thoughts. That little girl was the world to him. Everyone knew that as well as how deeply he grieved for his dead wife.

All of which merely made him more attractive.

More dangerous to her peace of mind.

Earn
FREE
REWARDS
Join
Today!
HarlequinMyRewards.com